THE LION AND THE MOUSE

SAMANTHA ALLARD

ACKNOWLEDGMENTS

Having the opportunity to write in Eve Langlais has been a great deal of fun. I want to thank her for opening this world up for fellow writers to build and expand. I've been a fan of her work since Kodiak Point. I also want to thank Jess Renee Ripley for doing a wonderful job at editing and leaving inspiring comments to spur me on.

And finally, to Rebecca Poole, who did an excellent job on the cover art.

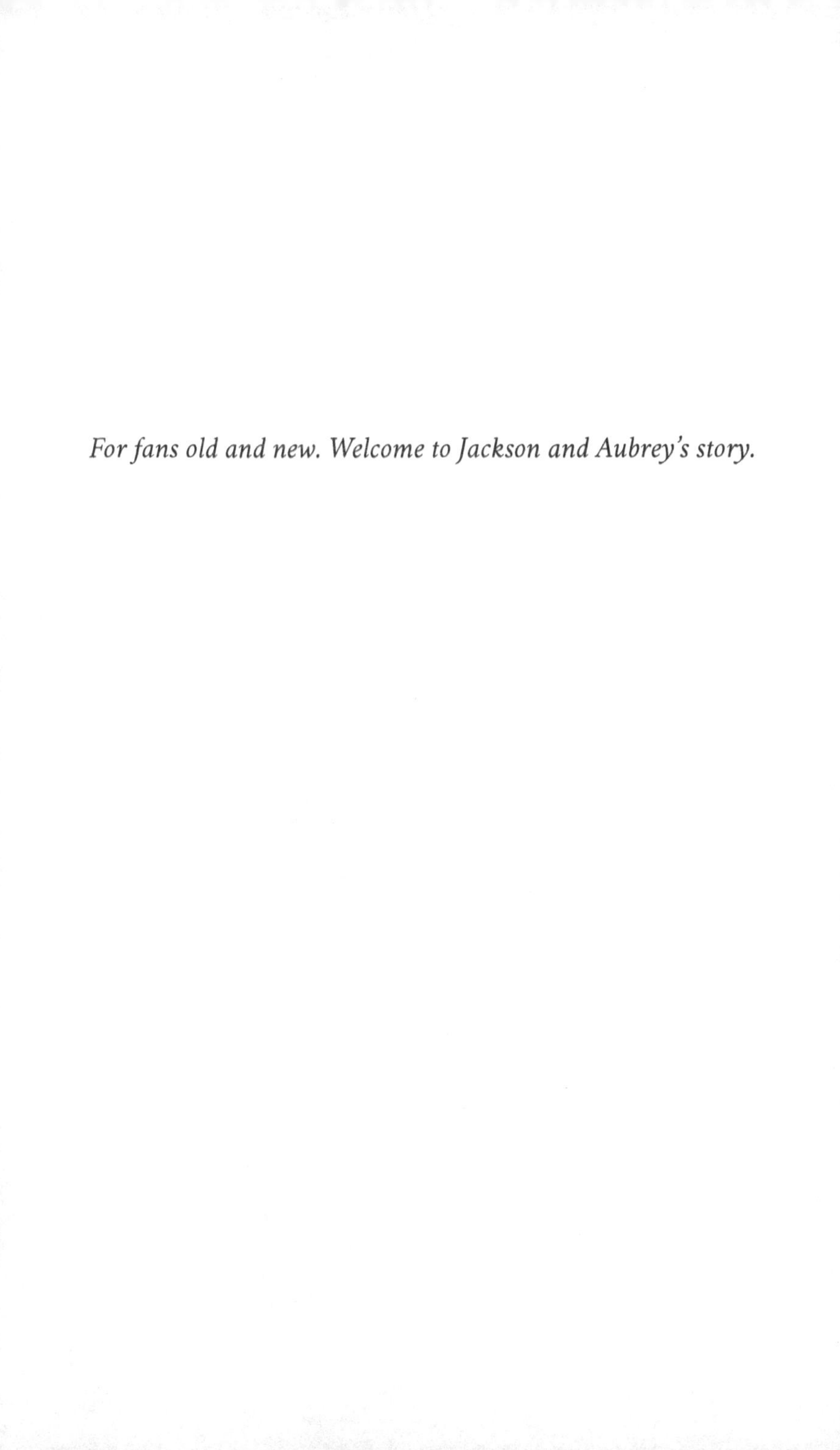

For fans old and new. Welcome to Jackson and Aubrey's story.

CHAPTER ONE

"WHY DIDN'T WE HAVE THIS DELIVERED TO US BY courier?" Jackson Holt, lion shifter, mumbled under his breath as he walked up the steps to the National Szechenyi Library. It was a beautiful summer day, and the streets were filled with people. Which meant he was hyper-alert, a trait picked up during his training to join the Furry United Coalition. A lazy agent didn't live for long.

"You know, a lot of people would have liked the impromptu trip to Budapest, instead of bitching about it." Neil Yun sighed, and the exasperated sound carried through Jackson's earpiece. It didn't matter that a thousand miles or so separated them. At that moment, his wolf friend could have been standing right next to him. Thanks to the glasses Neil had sent to Jackson, Neil could see everything he could.

"I'm supposed to be on holiday," Jackson grumbled.

He could count on one hand the downtime he'd had over the last two years. The life of an agent was an interesting one—full of a considerable amount of risk—and even if he loved it, he still needed a break. When was the last time he didn't have to worry about someone shooting him?

"I thought you'd be grateful for having a legitimate excuse to escape your mother's clutches."

Jackson pushed the door open and walked into the library's air-conditioned foyer. With his beige trousers and his white shirt rolled up to his elbows, he looked every inch the traveling tourist. At the base of his spine, where the specially designed gun holster rested, sweat had started to gather. He didn't need the gun, but it was easier to use than shifting into his lion form and scaring the locals. The existence of shifters was a closely guarded secret.

"You think my mother takes my work with FUC seriously?" Cassandra Holt was the CEO of Holt Industrials, a role that he was expected to step into when she left. It didn't matter that Jackson had cousins who'd gladly step into the role, like Ethan. However, Cassandra wanted to keep control and keep Jackson in the line of succession. "That woman holds a grudge like nobody's business." He strolled across the foyer, and a woman with wavy black hair down to her shoulders and dark red lipstick smiled at him from the front desk.

"Do you speak English?" Jackson asked in broken Hungarian. At least that was what he hoped he said. He spoke three languages fluently, and Hungarian wasn't one of them.

The woman's smile widened as she looked at him. "Yes, sir. How can I help you today?"

"My name is Jackson Parker," he replied, using a fake name that matched the falsified ID that he pushed across the desk to her. "I work for Professor Sanders, and I'm here to collect the book he requested."

The woman leaned forward, peering at his credentials and giving him an impressive view down her shirt, revealing her black laced bra. The move was a deliberate one, judging from the flirtatious look in her eyes. She ran her fingertip across the ID, her nails the same crimson shade as her lips.

"Oh, yes, Mr. Parker," she said in a husky voice while she batted her eyelashes at him. "How long are you in town for?"

"A few hours."

"Pity. If you had the time, I would have loved to show you our beautiful city."

"That's a shame," he said as he gave her a slow smile.

She tucked a strand of her hair behind her ear. "You can go through the door on the left and follow the hall to the door that takes you to our basement level. We would have had it ready for your arrival, but our librarian wanted to spend some time with the book before it left our possession."

He frowned. "And why is that?"

"Mr. Kovacs doesn't like foreigners." Her attention

shifted to the door then back to him. "Between you and me, he didn't even want to lend the book out. He doesn't think it'll be returned."

It wouldn't be, but the man didn't need to know his fears were justified. "It'll be in good hands, I promise."

Her gaze drifted lower. "Excellent hands. I mean, of course, it will. You're a librarian. Who would be better to act as a temporary guardian?" A blush crept over her face, and he grinned at her before he walked to the door that would lead to the basement.

"Did that woman seriously flash you?" Neil's voice sounded in his ear.

Jackson chuckled. "You saw everything I did."

"What must life be like to look like a Greek god?" Neil teased. It wasn't like the wolf shifter wasn't easy on the eyes himself, and he wasn't hurting for men and women who wanted to spend the night with him.

"You sure I need to be across the pond tonight?" Jackson glanced over his shoulder. He could think of worse ways to spend the night than in the company of a woman as beautiful as her.

"Yeah, FUC needs the book ASAP," Neil reminded him. "Now, keep your wits about you. We're not the only ones interested in it."

There were groups of people who worked against the interests of FUC. Some shifters just wanted to watch the world burn. Jackson never understood people like that, but he supposed the world required a certain level of balance. The shifter world had operated in secret for a long time, since humans had a habit of trying to destroy what they didn't understand.

Thankfully, those with better sense knew a war was the last thing anyone needed.

"You never told me why we need it," Jackson said as he walked through the door and down the hallway toward the next door marked *Basement.*

"That information is way above either of our paygrades," Neil informed him. "We have an expert on speed dial if we need their assistance, but they don't know everything either."

As soon as Jackson was in the stairwell, the hairs on the back of his neck stood on end. He hated cramped spaces.

A LINE OF LOW-HANGING LIGHTS DROPPED FROM THE ceiling, and Jackson had to walk to the side or risk head-butting them.

Panic bubbled inside of him. The incident from his childhood still haunted him. He'd been five and planned on hiding in the chest in his parents' bedroom. He'd wanted to jump out and scare whoever walked in, but he'd fallen asleep. When he'd tried to get out, he had quickly realized the chest had been locked.

"You okay there, buddy?" Neil's voice brought him back to the present.

Jackson breathed out, and slowly, his heart rate returned to normal. "I'm fine," he said through gritted teeth. When he reached the bottom of the stairs, he spied another man leaning over a table. There was a barely audible sound, and if he'd been human, he would have missed it. A camera? Why was the man taking photos of the book?

"Mr. Kovacs?"

There was the barest of warnings as the man at the table whipped around and pulled out a gun. Jackson dove for cover as the man fired off three muted shots. Whoever this man was, he was using a suppresser, meaning they were a professional. Definitely not the archaic librarian he was looking for. "Neil, tell me you got a good look at him."

"Running his face through our database. Give me a second."

Jackson kept low and crept around the stacks. His lion came to the surface, but he kept a tight leash on it. He would lose a lot of mobility if he shifted in such a confined space.

With his heightened senses coming to the forefront, he caught the scent of blood. It wasn't coming from him. The gunman swore and barked something into a walkie-talkie. Jackson couldn't make out the muffled reply.

That's when he found the librarian. The body of an elderly man with white hair had been left discarded on the floor. His eyes were open but unseeing, and a pool of blood had spread underneath him.

"Tell me who I'm fighting," Jackson hissed to Neil. He reached out and closed the dead man's eyes.

"He hasn't shown up," Neil growled in frustration. "But safe to say he's dangerous and you need to stop him before he leaves. Our mission is to obtain and contain the information found inside that book! There might be a chance he hasn't sent them yet. You need to destroy that camera."

Jackson peeked around the stacks. The man wasn't searching for him anymore, more focused on packing away a bag he slung over his shoulder. His weapon had been placed on the table next to him.

Jackson pulled his own gun free and darted out.

His target spun, lashing out with supernatural speed, and knocked the gun from Jackson's hand. A roar rumbled in Jackson's chest, and the man's face paled underneath his pencil-thin moustache.

"You don't scare me," he said as he edged away.

"The smell of piss in the air tells a different story." With his lion close to the surface, he recognized his opponent was another shifter—a lesser beast, for sure. "Now, why don't you hand the bag and camera over?"

"They'll kill me if I do."

Jackson raised an eyebrow. "And what do you think I'm going to do? Let you off with a stern warning? You killed a human."

The man's gaze shifted to where the librarian's body was, and he shook his head. "That had nothing to do with me."

Suddenly there was a loud crack—the sound of a gunshot!—and pain exploded across Jackson's shoulder. The man had a partner. *Crap, that was a rookie mistake to make.*

He ignored the pain and launched at the first man, who yelped out in surprise and terror. Jackson stopped short of grabbing him. Instead, he twisted his hips, dipped low, and delivered an uppercut with all his supernatural strength behind him. The man's eyes rolled up into his head, and Jackson picked up the dead weight and threw him over the table. He probably wasn't dead, but an unconscious attacker was better than one he needed to keep an eye on. Jackson grabbed the camera and checked the status of the upload. Whoever the man was, he hadn't had a chance to start it. Jackson removed the memory card and slipped it into the front pocket of his jeans. Then he smashed the camera.

Animal instinct told him to turn and face the new attacker, but the human part knew whoever they were, they hadn't hesitated in firing. He moved past the unconscious body to the other side of the table, noting the five open books laid out. Which one was he supposed to be collecting?

"You move quick," a distinctly female voice informed him.

The woman at the counter.

She'd dropped the flirty element to her voice. *Guess she's not interested in showing me the city anymore.*

"And you move quietly. I didn't even hear you

coming down the stairs." No gun and no straightforward way to close the distance between them. "Sorry. You're not getting the book."

"Not a problem. I have a contingency plan."

"I don't suppose you want to tell me who you're working for?"

"No." Her word was followed by the sound of a zipper and something being removed from a bag. "But if I can take out the legendary Agent Holt, my boss might not be too angry we lost the book. Goodbye, handsome."

The door swung closed behind her, and then there was a bang. Before Jackson could turn back to the books, he noticed smoke flooding the room, followed by the unmistakable aroma of fire. He looked to the old wooden stacks and the books, knowing there was no straightforward way to stop the spread.

"Is there any way to get out of here?" he asked Neil.

"I checked the floorplans before you went in. The only way out is the way you came."

Jackson looked at the books on the table. He could carry all of them out, but there was no telling if the mysterious woman waited to attack him in the lobby. Jackson needed his hand free for his gun.

"Neil, you better get the expert on the phone before this place gets burned to the ground. Also, scroll through the footage and find out who that woman was."

CHAPTER TWO

Aubrey Taylor had grown up with an intense love of books, mostly because she was the forgotten middle child, often left to her own devices. Not that it mattered. She lived a hundred lifetimes in the books she read.

Growing up, she wanted to be the hero. The knight who slew the dragon or the spy who traveled the world. It was why she'd wanted to become a FUC agent, but her parents had made sure she was aware that mouse shifters weren't built for that world. It was pointless for her even to apply to the Furry United Coalition Newbie Academy—FUCN'A for short.

So instead, she'd gone to school to become a librarian and had scored an assistant position at the Academy.

Which had been exciting enough until a week ago, when she had an unexpected phone call. One she had written off as a prank.

"Are you the Ms. Taylor, who wrote the paper on the forgotten texts of Miklos Bathory?"

"That's me. Who is this?" She hadn't recognized the voice but that didn't mean it wasn't one of the many staff members or agents at the Academy.

"Brilliant, my name is Neil Yun. I work as an analyst with FUC."

The name sparked a memory. A wolf shifter, one who completed his training shortly after she'd started at the Academy. "I remember you."

"You do?" She could practically hear the disbelief in his voice. "I don't think we've ever met."

"I have a good memory. Now, why are you calling me about a forgotten Hungarian philosopher?"

The paper she wrote for the shifter community had been met with a mixture of skepticism and praise. Bathory's works from the medieval era could only be found in the collections of powerful men and women worldwide, none who felt inclined to share the knowledge they hid away. The theory was that Miklos Bathory had been the first to write about the existence of shifters, at the time known as *Isten Teremtményei*, Creatures of God.

"One of the books has been discovered. We need your help."

THE FOLLOWING DAY A PARCEL HAD BEEN DELIVERED TO her containing an earpiece and a small box to help boost the signal. There had also been a pair of glasses and a note asking that she not put them on until she was told to. A part of her thought it was still some kind of joke, but another, smaller, part of her wanted it to be true.

I'm really being asked to assist on a FUC mission!

She had been in bed when the phone rang.

"Ms. Taylor." Neil's voice greeted her. "Please tell me you've got the parcel at hand. I'm going to hang up, but I need you to insert the earpiece and tap it three times to activate it."

Aubrey scooted off the bed and rushed to the table by the window. With her heart racing, she retrieved the small round pebble and slid it into place. Then she tapped it. The seconds dragged until the silence was broken by a series of long beeps.

"Mr. Yun?"

"Reading you loud and clear. There's no time to explain. Please put the glasses on, and I will patch you through to our agent in the field."

She didn't know what to do with herself. Did she sit or pace her tiny bedroom? With the glasses on, the metal cold against her skin, she slipped on her dressing gown, not bothering to tie it closed.

"I hear you're our expert." The voice was a rumble. "I'm Jackson." She assumed it must be Agent Jackson Holt, a lion shifter from the same cadet group as Neil.

The pair had been close during their time at the Academy.

"Hi, Jackson. Aubrey here."

"Great. Can you see what I'm seeing?"

Something in the glasses changed. Instead of being in her bedroom, Aubrey's view shifted to a different place. A room full of smoke. The clarity of the glasses was amazing. It was like being in the same room as him.

However, the sight of so many damaged books hurt like it was causing her physical pain.

"I can see. Now, tell me what you need from me."

Jackson started to cough. "A new set of lungs at this rate."

How could he be joking at a moment like this?

"Um, I was under the impression it was actually my expertise on Bathory that would help—"

"Ah, yeah, here, check these out. Can you tell me which of these is likely from our man?"

The view from the glasses moved toward a table where five large books lay open. All of them were written in Hungarian, and though she was a little rusty, she could make out the words. She leaned forward then remembered she wasn't in the actual room with him.

"Can you look more closely at the third book?" The image became clearer. It looked like a book on botany with colorful flowers and details written in small, neat handwriting. "That's the one you need."

She noted how his hands stilled on it. "Are you sure?"

"Trust me." She could give him a full explanation, but

the way he kept coughing made her think that it would be better for him to rush out of there. She was, after all, the expert that *they* tapped to help, so he should be willing to take her at her word.

"Keep talking to me," Jackson said, picking up the book as the smoke started to overwhelm their vision. She could make out him slipping into a container, and then he snatched up a bag from the floor and slipped the book inside. Coughs racked his body, making Aubrey flinch. She watched helplessly as he moved and flung a door open.

"I don't know what to say."

"Anything. Like, tell me why you're sure about this book." He barely got the words out as he stumbled up the stairs.

"Miklos had a passion for flowers and secrets," she explained. "What he discovered about the shifter races was often hidden in codes. Those unfamiliar with this fact would have missed it. The language has evolved, but I know enough to get by."

Jackson's movements slowed. A few more steps and he would be out of the worst of it, but if he collapsed now? Their kind, from mouse to lion, could heal a lot of damage, but there was a chance he'd be overwhelmed.

"Jackson!"

"I'm still here. I just don't like enclosed spaces. Keep talking. Help me take my mind off it." She watched as his hands appeared on either side of him, pressed against the walls as he pushed forward.

"I thought this request was a prank," she revealed. The door was about six steps away. All he needed to do was push it open and breathe in the fresh air.

"Why?"

"Made more sense than FUC needing my help." It wasn't much of an explanation, but she barely knew the guy and wasn't in the habit of spilling secrets. "I work at the Academy. In the library."

"It's because of you that we got the book. I would never have thought of it being written in code."

"Thanks." She beamed with pride.

Jackson finally stumbled into another room, this time a lobby. The area was a hub of activity. People rushed toward him, carrying buckets, unceremoniously pushing him out of the way. He nearly lost his footing, but he didn't fall. Instead, he steadied himself on the wall. He didn't stop for long and headed for a side door.

As soon as he stepped into the sunlight, she felt like a weight had been lifted from her shoulders.

"Aren't you going to wait for emergency services?" she asked. "You really should have a doctor look at you."

"I'll be fine in a few hours," he said while he kept walking. "Also, I can't risk them taking the book. Considering what I had to go through to get it."

"I guess I should get off the line. You'll need to report in." Aubrey glanced at her watch. Had it only been minutes? It felt much longer than that. "I'm glad I could help."

"Maybe the next time I'm in the area, I can pop in

and say thank you in person. I remember there being a nice little pub in town."

The suggestion made her pause. Jackson Holt was built like a Greek god, with a mane of blond hair and a smile that caused all panties in a five-mile radius to combust. Many women would kill for a chance to spend time with the lion shifter.

"My job keeps me pretty busy," she said, refusing to get her hopes up. He was being nice, and even if he suggested it now, she doubted he'd follow through on the offer.

"We all have to eat, Aubrey; it doesn't matter how busy we are. We could at least share a meal." His voice was steady, his body already fighting off the smoke damage.

"Okay," she said, non-committal.

"Great, you need to tap the earpiece three times to have Neil take over again. I'll see you soon."

She followed his instructions, but as she tapped it for the last time, her ears were assaulted by a loud pop followed by a squeal of feedback, and she yanked the earpiece out. *What on earth was that?*

Aubrey rubbed her ear. She called into the Academy's command center and requested to be transferred to Agent Yun. Each second she waited for him to pick up, the feeling of dread grew in the pit of her stomach. Had something happened to Jackson?

She held on to the handset with both hands until he finally answered. "Mr. Yun?"

"I'm sorry, Aubrey. There's been a problem, and we need to get it sorted. Thank you for your help today. We couldn't have done it without you."

She was being dismissed. "Has something happened to Agent Holt?"

Neil sighed. "I'm sorry, but I can't talk about an active case." The phone went dead, and she stared at it in disbelief. Rage bubbled to life inside her, and she threw the phone, which cracked as it struck the wall. She closed her eyes and rubbed her palms against them.

She rarely suffered from the outbursts that had plagued her during childhood anymore. On the prey side of the shifter world, mouse shifters weren't known for losing their tempers.

Was the popping noise the sound of a gun?

CHAPTER THREE

How was it possible that his butt cheek still stung? Jackson rolled onto his side and tried to take the pressure off it. The last thing he remembered was promising to see Aubrey soon. Then sudden and blinding pain. The doctor had joked if he wasn't such a hardass the bullet could have shot straight through and destroyed an artery or vein. Being a shifter wouldn't have mattered; Jackson would have bled out.

Thankfully, he was being released, and Neil was going to drop him off at his house. The first thing Jackson wanted to do involved a shower, shaving off his scruff of a beard, and devouring a meal that consisted of meat and potatoes. The food given to him in the medbay was barely tolerable for a meat eater.

Aubrey popped back into his mind. Neil had told him she had called to find out what happened, but he hadn't been able to answer any of her questions.

As soon as Jackson could, he knew he needed to see her. He owed her dinner as a thank-you.

The door swung open, and Neil strolled in. With the battered leather jacket, jeans, and band T-shirt, he couldn't have looked more out of place if he tried. His branch of the shifter world—wolves—was naturally inclined to work in the field, but Neil had always been more comfortable with computers. Besides, he hated guns, and FUC agents couldn't rely on their bodies being their only weapons.

"You're all signed out, dickhead. Let's get you out of here."

Neil had also been taking calls from his mother, so Jackson knew he owed him a drink—or five—for putting up with her.

"Thank god. Did you bring your motorcycle?"

"And subject you to sitting on your tender ass cheek? No, I brought the car. You can even lay on the back seat if you want to." Neil smirked.

"I think I'll manage," Jackson said as he collected his jacket and slipped it on. "I can't wait to get home."

"Are you expecting visitors?" Neil asked.

Jackson froze as he was about to get out of Neil's car.

The blue sedan in his driveway was instantly recognizable, but the seats were empty.

"That's my mother's car." For the love of God, he

couldn't deal with her right now. He nearly told Neil to floor it when he noticed two people sitting on the porch. They had already seen him.

He reluctantly got out, and his best friend followed, which Jackson appreciated. Cassandra Holt's temper was legendary, and nobody should have to face it alone. The man who stood to her left, dressed in a smart suit with his hands behind his back, was Heston. There wasn't a role the older man didn't fill. Chauffeur, body-guard, cook. The man had skills.

Jackson's mother was more than capable of looking after herself, but where Heston would disarm anyone he deemed to be a threat, Cassandra would kill in the blink of an eye. The lioness did what she had to do to protect the pride, and she regretted nothing.

His mother didn't move off the porch, and for a few awkward seconds, they just stared at each other. Did she know something had happened to him? He wouldn't put it past her to have people who reported to her about his whereabouts. A weary sigh escaped him; his butt had started to go numb.

"You plan on having a staring contest with her?"

"No," he said as he walked up the garden path and tried his best to hide the limp. "Afternoon." He stopped short of climbing the steps. She glared at him. His mother wasn't the most physically imposing woman with a barely five-foot-something body and short blonde pixie haircut. One way to describe her was petite, and she hated that word. Men might have been the pride leaders, but the females were the hunters. She made sure everyone was aware of that.

"Son." She stopped on the top step and scowled down at him. "I hear you've been in hospital."

"Just an accident at work." His mother knew he worked for FUC; the fact pissed the hell out of her. She couldn't get her head around the concept of the company's heir off saving the world. The more she pushed, the more he pushed back. He was a grown-ass adult; he had no intention of bending to the whim of his mother.

"Just an accident? Doubtful."

"Why are you here?" The numbness in his butt had turned into a cramp. Painkillers were useless when it came to shifters. Their bodies just burned straight through them. The throbbing pain in his butt cheek made it hard to hold on to his temper. "Not that it isn't nice to see you," he feebly added.

If she detected the lie, she didn't comment on it. "My assistant has called your phone several times, and you haven't answered. We were in the neighborhood and thought we'd visit. And to make sure you're aware your attendance is required in the office by the end of the week."

For a second, her words didn't click. For the longest time, they had avoided each other, so why did she want to make sure he'd be somewhere? Then he remembered. "The anniversary." His father had died ten years ago, and she always threw a remembrance ball. "I'll be there."

"Good." She turned her attention to Neil. "Which

means no assignments for him. He needs time to heal and to regain his peak strength and fitness. I won't have the other prides snapping at our heels because we don't show a united front."

His friend gave her a brisk nod, but even Jackson could see the sparkle of suppressed laughter behind Neil's grey eyes. "Yes, ma'am."

As the visiting pair walked down the steps, Heston nodded at him. The smile Jackson gave in return was genuine. Heston wasn't an alpha but a powerful beta who had worked for the Holt family since Jackson was a kid.

His mother stopped on the bottom porch step. "Heston, start the car. I'll be there shortly."

When the three of them were alone, she glared at Neil. "I wish to talk to my son... alone."

Neil shared a brief look with Jackson and, without another word, retrieved the key from under the mat and vanished inside the house.

"I want you to pick a wife at the event."

Her words took him completely by surprise. "I don't have a mate."

She waved her hand dismissively. "I didn't say mate. I said wife. I've invited the most eligible women in the city, and I want you to choose one. You might be more than happy to galivant around the world on your stupid causes, but I also need you to focus on continuing the family line."

There was no way she was giving him an ultimatum, was she? "And if I don't?"

"Then there will be consequences. All you need to do is pick one of the lionesses, get married, and get the woman pregnant. The pride will look after her and help raise the child. You have ignored your other responsibilities with the company, but I won't let you ignore this. It's time for you to stop being so selfish and start thinking about the future."

And with that, his mother stalked off, all five foot nothing of her in spiky heels. Jackson watched the pair drive off before joining Neil, who he found in the kitchen with two open beer bottles.

Neil gestured at the fridge. "There's some stuff in the fridge, but I figured you might want to order takeout on your first night home."

"Thanks," Jackson said, taking one of the beers.

"Did I hear all of that correctly?"

"You mean, did you hear my mother issuing foul ultimatums?" Jackson shrugged. "Then, yeah, you heard that."

"What are you going to do?"

Jackson took a long pull of his beer, savoring the bitter taste. "If thirty is too old to be adopted, there isn't much I can do."

"You'll let her marry you off?"

"Lions aren't the same as wolves. You guys have multiple alphas, but in my pride, all they have is me. I'm the leader, and I'm of marrying age. Things are expected of me."

"Don't you have cousins?"

Jackson nodded. "The one from my father's side of the family. Ethan, would be a perfect successor. He's a little younger than me. His mother, Aunt Celeste, moved out of the city when he was born. She didn't want my mother to perceive him as a threat to my future place in the company."

His mother was right to a certain point. Jackson was running away from his responsibilities. She had never understood why his work was important. He helped save the world in one shape or another, but she never seemed to be impressed. He had hoped for the mating urge to kick in, but it never had. For some shifters, it did, and for others, it didn't. "At least there's time to go somewhere first."

"And where's that?"

"To see Aubrey. I promised I'd take her out for dinner as a thank-you. I'm still on sick leave?" Neil nodded, but Jackson caught a flash of an emotion he wasn't expecting to see: panic. "Why do you look like you swallowed something unpleasant?"

The man finished his bottle and wiped his mouth with the back of his hand. "I don't know what you mean."

"You look guilty. What did you do?"

"I didn't do anything." He put the bottle down. "That's the problem. In my defense, I've been busy, and I didn't know you guys had hit it off enough to make plans. If I'd known, I would have…"

Jackson leaned on the counter and frowned. "You told her I was okay, didn't you?"

Neil looked bashful. "I'm sure she'd be really happy to see that you're still alive."

CHAPTER FOUR

It had been a rough couple of weeks. The people at FUCN'A had been completely useless and wouldn't give Aubrey an answer as to what happened to Jackson. The more she thought about it, the more confident she became that the sound she'd heard had been a gunshot.

She had gone through her job as if she'd been trapped in a dream she couldn't wake up from. She sat in her office and went over her list again. There was supposed to be a delivery of books in a couple of days, and for the life of her, she couldn't remember what they were.

The library at the Academy was her favorite place to be, from the smell of old books to the sound of students walking between the stacks. There was something about holding a book, the comfortable weight and the feel of history there. A computer tablet, soulless and impersonal, didn't have the same effect.

When she was finished for the day, she slipped the inventory list into her bag and stepped into the dull evening light. Why hadn't she been able to push Jackson out of her thoughts?

The heir to the Holt Corporation, who no one thought would want to train to become an agent. He'd spent his years at the Academy proving everyone wrong. She had often caught sight of him as he walked across the campus. How the beams of light caught the golden strands of his hair, his powerfully built body, and enough charm to make an old woman blush.

She bit her bottom lip.

Okay, she wasn't immune to those charms herself. Even if they'd never talked, even if she'd been there to train as an agent herself, they never would have been friends. Aubrey had grown up in a cottage, the middle child, and often overlooked by her parents, while Jackson grew up surrounded by money, able to do anything and get whatever he wanted. It frustrated the hell out of her. He was the prime example of having his life handed to him on a silver platter.

It should have made him an asshole, but instead, he was someone who wanted to save the world. It was hard to hate someone like him. It wasn't his fault he was built to be the perfect agent and she wasn't even allowed to try.

And now something had happened, and nobody would tell her what. Why would they? She wasn't anyone important. Wasn't a member of whatever task force had been on the Bathory case. She'd been only a one-off special guest for the mission. That didn't mean they owed her any intel.

Anger grew in the pit of her stomach, the strong emotion bitter and unmistakable. She wanted to hide away from the world. It was easier than facing what bothered her.

Aubrey reached her car, yanked the door open, and threw her bag into the backseat.

Instead of entering her car, she slammed the door closed and peered around. The Academy grounds were mostly empty, the students relaxing after a long day of training, so nobody would see her meltdown.

She took a deep breath and then yelled at the top of her lungs. The outburst was a coping mechanism taught to her by the therapist her parents had sent her to see. She screamed until her throat was raw then collapsed to the cold hard ground. Her animal wanted out, but mouse shifters weren't like other shifters. They weren't fighters. If she gave in to the urge, she would find herself a target for something much larger than her.

"That was an impressive scream for someone so small."

A voice she recognized came from somewhere behind her. Aubrey scrambled to her feet and peered over the hood of her car. A man she didn't think she'd ever see smiled at her. A few weeks ago, he had been a voice in her head and then a memory.

Damn, the years were more than good to Jackson Holt.

His blond hair was slightly longer, curled at the edges, and his usually amber eyes were a dark shade of blue, probably because he was wearing contacts. She slid down to the ground as her cheeks burned and her heart raced.

Maybe if she was quiet, he would just leave. There was a chance he didn't even know who she was. Her mortification made room for a feeling of relief to sweep over her.

He's okay.

"Aubrey?" There was the sound of movement on the other side of her car, and she fought against the irrational urge to sneak around to the other side and run away from him.

Before she could, she noticed Jackson's Converse Chuck Taylors, white with red stripes. Her gaze shifted up, and she noted his black jeans, the rich blue T-shirt, and the leather jacket.

He offered his hand, and she slipped hers into it. Heat spread from her fingers down to her toes as he helped her to her feet. Still, she didn't meet his gaze. She was acting like prey, and she hated those deeply ingrained instincts with every fiber of her being.

With gritted teeth, she pushed her insecurities aside and met his bemused smile.

"I'm Jackson. You must be Aubrey, you look just like your FUCN'A profile photo. It's good to finally meet you." He didn't let go of her hand.

"You're okay."

"Yeah, I'm sorry I couldn't get in contact with you earlier." The softest pressure was on the skin above her thumb, and she glanced down. He was rubbing his thumb against her hand. The movement was intimate, and sparks of pleasure shot through her.

Did he have any clue about the effect he had?

"It's been two weeks." Aubrey tugged her hand free. She needed to think, not be swept up in the presence of such a powerful man.

He had the decency to look a little bashful. "I'd be more than willing to discuss this over dinner."

The dinner. The one she thought wouldn't happen. Something offered in the heat of the moment.

She wanted to accept what happened and be happy he was okay, but she couldn't. "I thought you were dead." Her voice was hard and unyielding. "It's been two weeks with no word at all."

"Aubrey—"

She was starting to repeat herself, but her mind raced as if it had a life of its own. "You know what, I'm good. I've got stuff to do." She yanked her door open and glared at him.

"Aubrey!"

"I don't know what you expected to happen. Did you want this to play out differently? FUC stonewalled me when I tried to find out what happened to you." She got into her car and slammed the door with more force than was strictly necessary.

Anger swelled inside of her, an emotion so fierce it

was bitter on her tongue. She knew she was being irrational, but as she put her car into gear, she figured she didn't care. The sooner Jackson left, the better she would feel.

Jackson watched Aubrey drive away. Everything had happened so fast he didn't have time to react.

Aubrey had shifted from relief to barely contained rage in the blink of an eye, but there was something besides the mouse's anger that affected him. A tingle just at the base of his skull that started when they touched. A feeling he had never experienced before.

He crossed his arms, still rooted to the spot. Neil had informed him she was a mouse shifter, which had colored his expectations. A librarian and a small, demure creature? He had expected large round glasses and a homely appearance. Someone quiet, demure... predictable. He certainly hadn't expected an absolutely sexy woman screaming into the air with abandon. Her dark hair was pulled up into a bun, and even if she had curves, she buried them under clothes too big for her frame, like she was purposely trying to hide.

Neil had told him she'd worked at the Academy around the same time he'd been training there, but Jackson didn't remember her at all. Their paths should have crossed at least once or twice.

"Are you okay there?" A bubbly female voice jolted him out of his daze.

"I'm good."

"Well, as I live and breathe. Jacks! What are you doing here?"

The nickname took him by surprise, and he turned to face the newcomer. Miranda Brownsmith, dressed in a pair of high cut shorts and a crop top with her blonde hair pulled up in a high ponytail, was instantly recognizable. Jackson stumbled back as she leaped at him, pulling him into a tight hug. For someone so small, she was strong, and he was sure if she continued to hug him, she might crack his ribs.

When she finally let go, Jackson stepped away and rubbed his side. "I'm just visiting for a couple of days. I didn't expect to see anyone I know."

"Just here to see Alyce Cooper." The Director of FUCN'A was a formidable woman and not an easy one to forget. She shifted into a black llama and had a "fuck with me and see how long you survive" attitude.

Miranda, on the other hand, was the opposite. Some hadn't liked the fact a bunny wanted to be an agent, but she proved herself worthy of the title countless times—especially when they saw her in her oversized saber-toothed-bunny form! Now she led many different task forces, was happily married to a bear, and settled down with a kid. No, two kids… or was it three now?

"So, what are you doing here?"

"I was supposed to be taking Aubrey out for dinner." He glanced in the direction that her car had vanished. "She's a bit pissed at me, though. So, it's probably not going to happen now."

Miranda's eyes widened. "You're going on a date with Aubrey Taylor?"

It didn't surprise him that she recognized the name. Jackson might not have remembered the stunning brunette, but that didn't mean she didn't have friends at the Academy. Besides, Miranda knew everyone. She was just that kind of person.

"How do you even know her? You didn't go here together. She didn't attend the Academy as a student. Something about her parents forbidding it."

"Yeah, as I understand it, Aubrey worked as an assistant librarian around the time Neil and I were here. She's nice, though. Helped us out on a recent case. Why did you look surprised when I mentioned her name?"

"Because she's never really showed interest in anyone."

"Considering how she stormed off when she saw me, I doubt she's interested in me." He wanted to be wrong, but he could read a person, and she hadn't bothered concealing her anger. It shouldn't have mattered if she changed her mind, but he wanted to know more about her.

"I guess you don't have much experience with women not falling at your feet when they lay their eyes on you. Come on, let's get a coffee with a slice of carrot cake."

"Any excuse for cake," Jackson said with a chuckle and started to follow Miranda to the cafeteria.

CHAPTER FIVE

They ended up sitting at a table close to the window. The cafeteria was a hub of activity. The cadets lived on campus, so instead of closing after the daytime shifts, the staff kept the cafeteria open all hours.

Jackson had enjoyed the time he spent at the Academy. His mother had made her displeasure known on multiple occasions, but he had done his best to ignore her. His whole life had been planned out for him, and the day he left home had fractured his relationship with her beyond repair. He would say it broke his mother's heart if he thought she had one. After his father died, it was like she locked it away. He always knew he had obligations he was expected to fulfill. The weight of them was heavy on his shoulders.

There was time to worry about all of that later.

For now, he focused on his friend, a small fork practically overflowing with soft carrot cake poised at her lips. "You're limping. What happened?"

He shrugged. "I got shot in the ass with a big gun. Torn a lot of muscle, and it's taking its sweet time to heal."

"What case were you on?"

Typically, agents weren't allowed to talk about assignments. Since Miranda was in the same line of business and ranked higher than him, Jackson saw no problem discussing details with her. "You heard about the Budapest mission?"

"It came up on my desk." The impressive balancing act between cake and fork disappeared between her lips, and she took a minute to savor the flavors before continuing. "It was time-sensitive, and you were the closest agent. Sorry for pulling you off your holiday."

"Don't worry about it." He shook his hand, dismissing her apology. "Anyway, I managed to stop someone who was taking photos of the book, but a second intruder, a woman who posed as a secretary, set fire to the library before I could identify the book we needed. Aubrey was the specialist they had on speed dial. It's because of her we got what we needed."

"That doesn't explain why you're here."

The corner of his mouth twitched. "We were talking about meeting up when I got back. I got as far as the Danube, and I wasn't focusing on my surroundings like I should have been. I thought the woman must have fled the scene. I didn't think she might follow me and try to snatch the book I managed to make it out with."

Miranda winced. "She got the drop on you."

"That's putting it lightly. If I hadn't managed to throw myself into the river, she would have taken me out."

"All this for a book?"

"A pretty important one. Anyway, you remember Neil Yun. He forgot to tell Aubrey I was alive. I thought she would be a little happier to find out I was okay. Instead, she was angry."

"It's not my place to tell you her secrets," Miranda said, finishing her cake and leaning back in her chair with a smile. "Her file isn't sealed, but you know that's all kept confidential. What I can tell you is the girl has issues. She wanted to become an agent, but her parents stopped her application to the Academy. She's super smart, not genius level but close."

"Why would her parents stop her?"

"Not sure. It might have also been a decision by the higher-ups. You know how much they love us *weaker animals*," she said with quotation marks. Jackson had heard Miranda's story before. Due to a genetic abnormality in her family line, she shifted into a bunny that looked like the product of a drunken one-night stand between a gorilla and a sabertoothed tiger. It had been a closely guarded secret for a long time.

"What do you think I should do?"

She shrugged. "If you like her, I say go for it. If her

upbringing was anything like mine, she's lonely. That can be depressing as hell." A wide grin spread across her face. "Not everyone has the same sunny, no-quit attitude as me to combat that shit."

"She doesn't live on campus, does she?"

"Full-time staff don't. She has a small cottage on the outskirts of Nonamesville. Take the road through the town, and you'll find her."

Aubrey had spent twenty minutes on her living room floor, dressed in multi-colored leggings and a workout top, her legs crossed and her eyes closed.

Losing my temper is pointless. It never accomplishes anything.

She ran the mantra through her head. Who had ever heard of a mouse with a problem holding on to her temper? The feeling of anger gave way to a dull throb of regret. She had been happy to see Jackson was okay, but rationality had given way to the sneaky voices in her head. She wasn't good enough.

Books never made her feel that way. There was a certainty to written words. A clear start, middle, and end to every story. She got back to her feet and brushed down her leggings. She hadn't been able to get work done in the library, but now that she had answers—even if a little delayed—she could focus on something else.

Anything but the tall, handsome man who had traveled miles to see her. He looked exactly how she remembered him.

She decided to make herself a cup of chamomile tea. The kettle was set up in front of the window, and she'd always enjoyed looking out into her garden and the fields beyond it. The sun had started to set, and the dying beams of light cast everything in a warm glow.

She breathed in the heady aroma of her cup of tea. As she was about to turn around, something darted across the field. A large, dark shadow moved through the tall grass. Aubrey put her cup down and leaned forward to get a better look. Being this close to the Academy meant random sightings of animals that weren't native to the area were common. There were rules, though.

The trainees weren't supposed to pull any stupid stunts for one. What would happen if a human saw a tiger or wolf? It would go viral, for sure.

What could she do? The students didn't take her seriously. Did she need to call Director Cooper?

Knock, knock.

She frowned. She never had visitors. Christ, had the trainee agents grown bold enough to try a game of knock, knock, dash?

Aubrey stalked across the room and flung the door open. The glow of the setting sun made her visitor's blond mane take on an amber hue. A slow smile spread across Jackson's face, his gaze hungry as he took in her clothes.

"What are you doing here?" Aubrey snapped, holding back on her instinct to slam the door in his face.

"I think we got off on the wrong foot."

"How do you even know where I live?" Aubrey took a step back. She wasn't scared of him. Okay, she was a little scared. The way her heart raced and her face grew warm was something she wasn't used to. She was aware of him in a way she had never experienced before.

"Miranda pointed me in the right direction. Are you okay?" He studied her. The blue contacts had been removed to reveal his natural color.

"I'm fine," she snapped.

"Are you sure? You look a little flushed."

Most shifters were experts in body language, able to read someone on a level a human couldn't even imagine. Jackson had to know the effect he had on her, an effect he had on any woman within a mile radius of him. "I thought I saw something in the field. Was that you?"

His brow furrowed. "No, show me where you saw it." There was something about his tone that suggested he expected her to give in to the request.

She gestured for him to enter and closed the door behind her. "It's probably nothing. I was making a cup of tea, and something caught my eye. Then you knocked on the door." She kept her home tidy, but she could count on one hand how many people had set foot in it besides her. Jackson peered through the window then opened the door and stepped into the garden. He moved like a predator, all coiled energy and barely contained power.

"Does it happen a lot?"

"A few times, mostly near the start of the year when the recruits start. Wait a minute. What do you think you're doing?" She watched in horror as he shrugged out of his jacket. Then he pulled his T-shirt over his head and dropped it to the ground in one smooth motion. The muscles in his back rippled, and Aubrey's mouth went dry as other parts became wetter. As his hands went to the top of his jeans, she spun around.

"I'm going to check it out. My senses are better in my other form. I'll be able to pick up on the scent. Then when I go back to the Academy in the morning, I'll be able to match it with one of them."

More clothes hit the ground. The urge to have a peek nearly overwhelmed her. She bit her bottom lip and clenched her hands into fists.

"I'll be back in a minute."

She counted to ten and then turned around, watching as the lion padded through the gap where the gate should have been.

CHAPTER SIX

Being around Aubrey brought out a playful side Jackson hadn't indulged in a while. Fortunately, as soon as she mentioned seeing something in the field, he pushed down the urge to tease her. His inner animal hadn't liked the idea in the slightest. No, his lion demanded to stake a claim on the mouse shifter. Whoever wanted to scare her didn't know who they were dealing with.

The way Aubrey blushed at the sight of him didn't escape his notice.

She liked what she saw.

And whoever invented leggings needed to get a medal. The material was awesome. It hugged every curve on her body. Ones he wanted to nibble on.

He kept himself low to the ground and crept forward. If anyone was still in the field, they were stealthy. Jackson closed his eyes and rested his head on his large paws. It wasn't easy to pinpoint a scent. Multiple critters roamed the field. All of them had scattered when he entered. He ruled out things that were pure animals. Shifters were a blending of the two, their scent unique.

There was a rustling of movement to his right. It hadn't been close, but since the wind shifted, a scent reached him. He launched himself in the direction without a second thought. Whatever he hunted was fast, and he couldn't place what or where they were. They darted to the left but then vanished deeper into the long grass. Jackson bounded after them. If it was one of the trainees, they were going to be in a world of trouble when he got a hold of them.

The tall grass was easy for them to disappear in, but they wouldn't be able to hide forever. Jackson sprang forward with his powerful hind legs and identified the figure as a jaguar just as he noticed the parked car the cat shifter was headed toward.

The jaguar was too far ahead, and as Jackson followed, he realized there was someone waiting behind the wheel.

The jaguar leaped into the open door, and the car sped off, the wheels kicking up dust and masking the license plate. Jackson tried to focus on the combination of numbers and letters, but it wasn't easy. He knew he wouldn't be able to keep up with them. He stopped and turned back to the field.

When he returned to Aubrey's cottage, he stopped at

the back door and shifted back into his human form. He retrieved his clothes from the back of one of the garden chairs—*how nice of Aubrey to pick them up and place them there*—and slipped his jeans back on. Aubrey had been uncomfortable with his approach to nudity, and it wasn't polite to give the woman an eyeful she didn't want.

As he stepped into her home, he saw that she hadn't strayed from the kitchen. She leaned against the counter with a cup in hand, and the looks she gave him set a shot of desire straight to his groin. Did she have any clue about the effect she had on him?

Aubrey was still dressed in the leggings and workout top; the scoop of the neckline revealed the straps of her lacy bra. Whatever sport she'd been doing when he knocked on the door hadn't been strenuous enough to require a sports bra. If he looked hard enough, he could make out the white lace that cupped her breasts. When he looked up, the corner of Aubrey's mouth kicked up into a smile.

"Did you find what you were looking for?"

Jackson was usually much more suave around women, but Aubrey had thrown him through a loop when they first met. Now he was stumbling to regain his footing. "I've seen plenty of things I wouldn't mind seeing more of."

Her brow furrowed. "I'm talking about whoever was in the field."

"Me too." He also wanted to slip the workout top

over her head, pull down the cups of her bra, and lick and tease her nipples. His cock grew harder. Jackson pulled his shirt on, the length long enough to cover the hard length of his arousal.

"Right." The word was long and drawn out. She didn't believe him, but the smell of her desire was thick in the air. Had she caught sight of him as he shifted back into his human form? Had she liked what she'd seen? "Did you see who it was?"

"A black jaguar. Do you know any?"

She shook her head. "We'll have to talk to personnel." Silence descended between them. "Did you want a drink? I don't keep alcohol in the house, but would you like coffee or tea?"

At least she wasn't trying to kick him out. "You know what I want?" He moved toward her. "Do you know what has played on my mind ever seen I had your voice in my ear?"

Suddenly there was only a sliver of space between them. Her pupils drowned out her irises, and she looked up at him, so small in comparison to him. She looked like a deer caught in headlights.

"What do you want?"

He cupped her chin. "I want to take you to dinner."

Her skin was hot underneath his hand. "I thought you were going to say something else," she replied breathlessly.

A part of him wanted to trace a path across her full bottom lip with his thumb, to feel the soft plump flesh there. Another part wanted to place her on the table and free her from her leggings. The smallest voice, the one of reason, knew it was unwise. He hadn't traveled all this way just to hook up with her and forget about the responsibilities that waited for him back home. For a second, she leaned forward, her lips parted in a silent invitation.

He gave her a half-smile before he stepped away, breaking contact with her. His lion roared in displeasure. The intense reaction didn't surprise him. They were usually of one mind when it came to bed partners. This was the first time they weren't in complete agreement.

"We better get going."

THEY ENDED UP IN THE HUB. AUBREY MIGHT HAVE SPENT the last three years at the Academy, but she'd never been to the shifter-owned bar. The bustling space was a place someone went to with friends, and since she didn't have any of those, she hadn't seen the point.

Jackson, on the other hand, was greeted immediately. If there was any doubt about his popularity during his time training, that doubt was dismissed at that moment. Why had she even said yes to this? It felt like everyone was looking at her, wondering why the golden boy had chosen her.

He led her to one of the free tables and pulled out a

chair for her. Age-old resentment built inside of her, but she gritted her teeth and sat.

"Are you okay?"

"I'm fine."

He raised an eyebrow. "You want to unclench your jaw and try that again?" Suddenly he reached out and touched her hand. Awareness shot through her. "You don't like people, do you?"

Something was soothing about the way he touched her. How was it possible that one simple thing could chase the doubt away? She closed her eyes and took a deep breath. "It's not that," she admitted, looking at him. "You wouldn't understand."

"Try me."

It wasn't even a question, but she pulled her hand free. "I've never been here before. What's good?"

He leaned back into his chair, and the look he gave her sent shivers up her spine. She got a strong feeling he wouldn't just drop the line of questioning. "The last time I was here was two years ago. Work has me traveling all over the world." He pulled a menu toward him. "Doesn't look like much has changed. Burgers were always good. What do you like?"

"I'll have whatever you're having."

His lips curved into a half-smile, and he smirked. "I have a pretty big appetite. Do you think you can handle what I have?"

She'd seen his handful when she caught sight of naked him from her kitchen window as he returned from his hunt. The man's sex appeal was palpable and hard to ignore. With broad shoulders and a body that looked like he spent a fair amount of time in the gym, he towered over her. It wasn't intimidating but rather sexy as hell to know he could protect her.

"That sounds like a challenge."

AUBREY LAUGHED AT THE INCREDULOUS LOOK ON Jackson's face as she finished the last of her onion rings. In the end, he had ordered the full stack of pancakes, three quarter-pound burgers with onions, lettuce, tomato, and the pub's house sauce. They both ended up with bottles of chilled beer.

"Well, I've always been a firm believer a woman should finish first."

Her face went hot, and she nearly choked on her last bite. "You really shouldn't say things like that when someone is eating." She picked up her drink and took a sip.

Jackson put a hand on his chest, his eyes wide in mock innocence. "I don't know what you're talking about."

"Of course, you don't." She had done her best to ignore the looks people were giving them. Mostly the women who looked at Jackson with hunger in their eyes. "This has been fun," she said honestly. "Thank you for this."

"It wasn't a hardship." The seconds dragged out between them. "FUC owed me a holiday anyway."

"You could have spent it anywhere." Besides living with her parents and then her cottage, she had never traveled outside of the country. A pang of guilt hit her. "I'm sorry you wasted some of that time here, with me."

He frowned. "Aubrey, there isn't anywhere else I want to be."

There was no way he could mean that. He just didn't want to hurt her feelings.

"You know," he continued, "I wish I could punch the asshole who made you believe you weren't worthy of people's time."

"I've got to head back now." She didn't know what to say to that, but she picked up on the honesty in his words. "I've got work in the morning."

"We also need to talk to the office about the jaguar on your property."

She'd been having such a fun time she'd forgotten about the mysterious shifter.

CHAPTER SEVEN

They'd traveled separately to get to the Hub, but Jackson still followed her back to the cottage to make sure she got home safe. She had tried to say she'd be okay, but the incident from earlier still played on his mind.

He also enjoyed her company and didn't want the night to end. He planned on staying in the motel, but he hadn't booked a room. If they were full, which happened even in a small town, he might be able to snag a room at the Academy.

He walked her to her door, and she stopped before going in, looking up at him in a way that had him absentmindedly tucking a loose strand of hair behind her ear. Christ, he liked her. A beautiful woman filled with contradictions.

She bit her bottom lip, and she looked down at the ground, mumbling something he didn't catch.

"What was that?"

"I can't think straight when you touch me."

"Do you want me to stop?"

She shook her head.

There were a million reasons why kissing her was a bad idea. Like the fact that his mother wanted him to settle down and find a nice lioness.

He pushed the thought to the back of his mind and cupped Aubrey's cheek, guiding her face up. There was uncertainty in her dark gaze, but it warred with desire. A better man would turn away and leave, but Jackson didn't want to be the better man.

There was a good height distance between them, so he leaned down as her lips parted. The kiss was sweet, chaste, but as she hesitantly put her arms around his neck and he lifted her off the floor completely, it became something more primal.

She wrapped her legs around his waist, and he pushed open the cottage door. He teased the seam of her lips, and she opened for him with a moan.

"Where's your bedroom?"

"Door on the left," she replied breathlessly.

Their lips didn't part until he laid her down on the bed, not wasting time trying to locate the light switch. His eyes adjusted to the darkness, and he made sure not to put his full weight on her. Being with her was already pure insanity in the best of ways.

The way she trailed her nails down his back as she nibbled his bottom lip made his lion roar in approval.

He cupped her ass, her leggings the only barrier between them. The heat between her legs practically burned him.

"Are you wet for me, sweetheart?"

She nodded and rocked her hips as if she was trying to generate more friction.

"Stop that," he said, kissing her and nipping her bottom lip. Her body stilled.

"The only one getting you off tonight is me." The words rumbled in his chest. "Do you understand?"

"Yes."

"Are you fond of these leggings? There's something I've been wanting to do to them since I first saw you in them."

When she shook her head, he moved until he was between her legs. He ran his hands from her ankles up to her thighs then grabbed the waistband and ripped. The material gave way under his hands and revealed her pale, naked body underneath. He groaned in surprise at her lack of panties. "You're so beautiful."

"You don't have to say that." He noticed her turn away from him. Her dark hair was loose around her shoulders, creating a soft dark halo.

"I don't say anything I don't mean." He pulled his T-shirt over his head, and her gaze darted back to him.

There it was, the volatile side, the one at war with the vulnerable side of her personality. Jackson closed the distance between them, claiming her lips with another searing kiss and pulling her up while he lay on his back, guiding her to straddle him.

"I don't usually do this." The look in her eyes was uncertain, though she settled in place.

"That's okay," he told her, his hands on her hip. "Take off your top. Let me see all of you."

Her top and bra were quickly discarded onto the bedroom floor. Her moves were quick, but as she wrapped her arms around herself, he knew she was nervous. Did she think he might judge her?

He sat up and slowly uncrossed her arms. She offered little resistance. Without a moment of hesitation, he started to tease her nipples. She rocked against his cock, which was barely restrained by the confine of his jeans. The movements were maddening in the best way.

All he wanted to do was sink into her wetness.

To mark her as ours.

The random thought popped into his head, and he lost his rhythm.

Oh fuck, it can't be that.

Aubrey hadn't noticed his distraction, or she was past the point of caring. Her movements became more frantic. She was close to her release. Jackson pushed the thought to the back of his mind, like all the other things he couldn't deal with. He focused on lying back and guiding Aubrey higher and higher until she was perfectly placed above his mouth. She leaned forward, her hands braced on the wall as he curled his arms around her thighs and tasted her.

The cry that escaped her was like music to his ears.

He made sure to keep his lion under tight control. He didn't want to end up hurting her. With wanton abandonment, she ground against his hungry mouth. Another cry, and her whole body became taut as her essence coated his tongue. He kept a hold of her as she slumped against the wall, and as he looked up the line of her body, their eyes met.

Mate.

━━━━━

AUBREY WASN'T IMPULSIVE. HER LIFE HAD BEEN PLANNED out even before she knew what that meant. There had always been a part of her that wondered what her life would have been if she rebelled against her parents' wishes. They certainly wouldn't have approved of Jackson. She lay with her head on the chest of a man who had made her see stars... with his tongue.

He ran his hand up the length of her body like he couldn't get enough of touching her. She found herself doing the same until her hands rested on the button of his jeans. The feel of the top of his erection as it bumped against her palm made her blush.

"Do you want me to take these off?" he asked.

She had known him for only a short amount of time, but she quickly figured out he wouldn't do anything to make her feel uncomfortable. "Yes."

Jackson shuffled around a little and kicked off his jeans. His cock sprang free. The last time she had seen it, when he'd stripped before shifting, it had been soft but still impressive. Now it was rock-hard and larger than she originally thought. He put his hands behind his head. Aubrey tentatively reached out and brushed her fingers against the smooth skin.

"You okay there, sweetheart?" he asked.

Her face went hot. Christ, she was pathetic. "I'm fine."

Jackson sat up, held on to her waist, and pulled her against his lap. Not for the first time, she marveled at his strength. All shifters were strong, but he made it seem so effortless. "I know the first time someone sees it, it can be a little intimidating." He whispered the words against the curve of her neck. "You're in control here, and I know you're wet enough to take all of me. I'll slide right in, but we can take our time. Let you adjust."

He nibbled her earlobe, and she rubbed herself against him. "It'll be a form of torture, but I can't wait until my cock is slick with your juices."

"You certainly have a way with words."

"It shouldn't be a surprise since you've already experienced what I can do with my tongue."

Aubrey reached between them and slowly guided him between her legs. She moved him against her overly sensitive lips, watching how his eyes drifted closed. Then she lowered herself down. Her body stretched to accommodate him, and the pain swiftly gave way to pleasure. When he was fully inside of her, they started to move in a gentle rise and fall. This wasn't what she had been expecting. She opened her eyes and noticed he was watching her.

"Are you okay?"

"I'm close."

He groaned and brushed a kiss across her lips. "I can feel it. You're so wet."

"Are you?" Her words were breathless, and she didn't sound like herself at all.

"Yes," he replied, his thrusts becoming rougher. "Come for me, sweetheart. I'm not going to last much longer. You feel so damn good wrapped around me. I want to feel you come, to squeeze my cock tight as I explode inside of you."

His dirty words were all she needed to hear. She leaned back, his hands on her hips and her hands on his thighs. True to his word, he swiftly followed her, his fingers pressing hard enough into her skin that there would be bruises in the morning. She didn't care. She didn't mind him leaving a mark on her.

CHAPTER EIGHT

The heady aroma of coffee woke Jackson from his slumber. He couldn't remember the last time he'd slept so peacefully. Aubrey popped her head around the door, her cheeks turning pink at the sight of him. Any doubts he had about the night before were promptly forgotten. Her dark hair was a wild mess, and he loved the way her gaze swept over him: a mixture of possessive and needy.

He was more than ready to go another round with her.

"Morning." He smiled as he ran his hand through his mane of hair.

"I don't know how you like your coffee." The words left her in a wild rush. "I mean, do you want a drink? I've got to jump in the shower before I head to work."

"Before *we* head off to work," he corrected her. "I'm coming with you, remember?"

"You don't have to do that. Whoever they were, they haven't come back."

"Is it normal for the cadets to pull pranks on you?"

She glanced over her shoulder and stepped back into her bedroom. Jackson watched as she walked to her wardrobe and started to pull out clothes. "It's not pranks. I'm a little weird. The trainees like to make fun of me for it."

"We're all different. Why tease you?" He got out of the bed and started to pull on his clothes. He needed a shower, but he figured asking would be pushing his luck. There was a chance she would say yes to the sharing idea, but then nothing would get done. Except her, thoroughly, until she screamed out his name.

"You'll have to ask them." Her back was stiff. A touchy subject. Jackson dropped it.

"I'll go sort the drinks out while you jump into the shower. I need to make a phone call anyway." He buttoned up his jeans. "How about you tell me how you like your coffee, and I'll make it while you shower?"

Her brow furrowed as she studied him. "You don't have to do that."

"How about you stop dictating what I can and can't do and just tell me?" He crossed his arms, and they just stared at each other. "Out of all the possible battles, this is the one you want to win?"

He liked the way she looked in the morning with a small pair of boxers that cupped her butt cheeks and a pale pink vest top.

"How about this," he continued, fighting against the urge to close the distance between them. "You tell me how you want your coffee, or I'll feast on that sweet spot between your legs? You'll have to call in sick because I won't be stopping until your legs turn to jelly."

She squirmed in front of him, the tops of her thighs pressed together as she nibbled on her bottom lip. "White, two sugars."

"A normal man would be a little insulted you chose the coffee over a good fucking."

Her breath caught. "And what about you?"

The corner of his mouth twitched. "The day isn't over yet, sweetheart."

JACKSON PICKED UP HIS CUP OF COFFEE AND WALKED INTO the garden. He looked over the fields, wondering if the pranksters had made a reappearance but didn't see anything. He pulled his phone from his back pocket and brought up Neil's number. So much for promising himself he wouldn't call work.

The wolf shifter wasn't an early riser, so Jackson was surprised when he picked up immediately.

"Good morning, Neil."

"You better be on your motherfucking death bed," his friend growled in response.

"I'm alive and well, but I do have a question. You got enough working brain cells to give me an answer, or do you need coffee?" There was the sound of movement on the other side of the line. "I'm not interrupting something, am I?"

"Just my sleep," Neil said with a sigh. "Okay, what do you want to know?"

"I need a list of jaguar shifters who are currently enrolled in the Academy."

There was a pause, and he pictured his friend pondering the question. "Any particular reason why?"

"Saw one skulking about in the area. Going to head into the Academy and ask around, but if you can find a name for me, it'll save me some legwork." He sipped his coffee and noticed some movement in Aubrey's home. She was about to get into the shower.

The image of her body wrapped in a towel hit him hard. When was the last time he had an immediate reaction like this? It was like being a horny teenager all over again.

Mate.

The word snaked back into his mind and took hold. It shouldn't have been possible. A lion and a mouse weren't a good pairing, especially when he had a mother who wanted him to breed with a lioness. His mother would have a heart attack

He smiled and shook his head.

"There isn't one," Neil confirmed.

For a second, Jackson didn't think he heard correctly. "What do you mean, there isn't one? I saw them with my own eyes. I caught their scent."

"Sorry, mate, I've got the database in front of me. No records of a jaguar in the cadet roster, nor the other residents, any of the staff, or instructors. Let me get some coffee, and I'll do a wider search. They might not have updated their system yet. I'll get back to you."

The phone went silent, and Jackson tucked it into his pocket. If it wasn't a student, who was it?

———

Aubrey had been in a state of constant awareness since she stepped into the shower. She didn't want to leave Jackson by himself for too long. As she thought of the lion shifter, she closed her eyes and rested her forehead against the steam-covered door. She had never had a one-night stand before, and she didn't know what she was supposed to do. Was this a fling? Why did it feel like more than that?

Under normal circumstances, she never would have met Jackson, and in the space of a single day, she had experienced the most mind-blowing sex of her life. She'd thought he would make his excuses and leave as soon as he woke up, but he hadn't.

She could still feel his hands on her, like his touch had branded her. A primal need built in the pit of her stomach, and as if it had a life of its own, her hand drifted between her legs. She was still tender, swollen, and pleasure shot through her.

Suddenly the shower door swung open, and she

jumped. She knew she should stop, but she continued to rub herself and cried out as she found her release. Jackson watched her with hooded eyes as he wordlessly took her hand and slowly sucked her fingers clean.

"Just like I remembered," he growled, and the sound made her stomach twist up in knots.

The spray from the shower head hit him, and his T-shirt stuck to his skin. With his free hand, he unbuttoned his jeans and pushed them to mid-thigh. Then he stepped under the shower with her. With one smooth motion, he pushed her back against the wall and thrust inside her.

Aubrey held on for dear life as the powerful lion shifter fucked her against the ceramic. She quickly adjusted to his size and cried out as another orgasm ravaged her. The urge to bite him took over, and she nipped his shoulder.

He grabbed her shoulders and pushed her against the wall, still buried inside of her, her legs around his waist. She rolled her hips, silently willing him to continue. The look in his eyes was all-consuming.

Mate.

The thought popped into her head. No, it couldn't be that. The goddess wouldn't be so cruel as to pair her with someone so unsuitable!

Suddenly he grabbed both her hands and pinned them above her head. The position should have made her feel vulnerable, but she felt protected, shielded by his body as he thrust inside her.

"You feel so good," he groaned.

So do you, she wanted to say. *You feel like home.*

"Faster," she moaned instead.

After that, it didn't take long for her to climax, and he roared as he followed her into his state of bliss. The grip on her wrists hurt, but it was a good pain. She barely noticed as Jackson cleaned and toweled her off. Then he pulled off his clothes and wrapped a towel around his waist.

For a second, she didn't know what to say. Did he feel the connection as well? Was it all in her head? There was a smile on his face, the look of a satisfied man. "I don't suppose you have a dryer I could use, do you?"

CHAPTER NINE

Aubrey had never been late to work before. She worked the early shift, though, so thankfully, there wasn't anyone waiting for her as she unlocked the door. The delivery would arrive in a few hours. Jackson had left her to go talk to someone since he was focused on finding out who was in the field yesterday. After everything that happened, she hadn't given it much thought.

She headed straight toward her office but stopped short of opening the door. There was a scent in her library, one which shouldn't have been there. A surge of anger swept over her. The library was her inner sanctum; besides her home, it was the place she spent the most time, surrounded by books. Most of them were untouched since the cadets had access to computers.

The door had been locked, but that hadn't stopped the intruder

She scanned the room until she identified their entry

and exit. She walked over to the open window and let her animal come close to the surface. It didn't matter that she was just a mouse; her senses were as heightened as the next supernatural creature. The unknown scent grew stronger.

From a casual look over the main library, nothing seemed out of place. Why would someone come in here and not touch anything?

She closed the window and headed back to her office. For a second, her eyes couldn't focus on the mess in front of her. She kept her office neat and knew where everything was. Now there were papers all over the floor. The drawers on her desk had been tugged out and the contents scattered on the floor. Even her coffee mug had been broken.

Aubrey closed her eyes and stepped out of her office, closing the door behind her. *What on earth is going on?*

***

THE FUCN'A RECEPTIONIST ONLY CONFIRMED WHAT Neil had told Jackson: there wasn't a jaguar shifter at the Academy. Was there a chance Jackson had been wrong?

As soon as he entered the library, he knew something was off. There was a strong scent at war with the delicate aroma of his mouse shifter.

He found her sitting on the floor of the library, her hands clenched in fists and her eyes closed.

"Aubrey? Talk to me, sweetheart." He knelt at her

side. She didn't open her eyes, and he noticed the smell of blood. Christ, was she hurt? Carefully he took her hands and noted the swell of red underneath her fingernails. "You're hurting yourself."

"I'm trying to keep myself under control, or I'm going to hunt down the person who did this."

"Did what?" He rose to his feet and peered into her office. It had been ransacked. Another prank? No, that didn't make any sense. It looked like someone had been searching for something. He returned to her side and asked, "Have you reported this to security?"

She shook her head. "No. They came in through a window." She opened her eyes, and they were pitch-black. Her mouse was close to the surface. There was something animalistic about her face, more angular. Mice weren't supposed to have problems with anger, but there was something different about her. She let out a shuddery breath. "I didn't want you to see me like this."

"It raises some interesting questions, but now isn't the time for any of them. Come on, we should report this to Alyce."

She fiercely shook her head. "No, this is my problem. I'll figure it out."

"You don't have to." He helped her stand. Suddenly his phone burst to life, and he pulled it free, and seeing that the caller was Neil, he answered it. "I'm in the middle of something. This is going to have to wait."

"Shame, I have information for you. You've got time for that, don't you?"

Jackson stepped away from Aubrey, who had started to look more like herself. "You found the jaguar?"

He caught the sound of his friend tapping something on a keyboard. "It isn't good news. We got a positive ID on the woman in Budapest. Layla Feyer. Jaguar shifter with ten confirmed kills to her name. Looks like you were lucky to survive your encounter with her. Most recent employer is known as the Broker. Unfortunately, we don't have much information about them."

"You think she's the mysterious shifter?"

"Jaguars are rare, and that's the animal she can shift into. It's too much of a coincidence."

"Why is she here?"

"The lost book, I'd wager. Maybe she followed you, or maybe they learned of Aubrey's research on Bathory and assumed she'd be in possession of the book. There are a lot of people who'd pay a ridiculous amount of money for one of Bathory's lost texts."

"Aubrey's office was ransacked. Looked like someone was searching for something."

"Is Aubrey, okay?" Neil asked, catching the harsh tone in Jackson's voice.

Jackson didn't elaborate, but then again, he didn't need to. They already knew what was happening. Bringing Aubrey in as the specialist on their case had drawn the attention of someone terrible.

"Hand me over to her." Jackson did what Neil asked and then went into Aubrey's ransacked office.

He opened the door and breathed in the unknown

scent. It was the same as the one from the field outside Aubrey's home.

Very carefully, he walked the perimeter, letting his lion come close to the surface. He was furious someone had invaded his mate's space. Images of tearing the jaguar woman limb from limb came to mind. His lion's intention was clear.

There was only one answer to someone who threatened their mate. A very final death.

He re-joined Aubrey in the main library, where she was arguing with Neil.

"I can't just leave." A pause.

"My whole life is here." She sighed. "No, of course, I don't want to die."

Jackson plucked the phone out of her hand. "Neil, I'll get her out of here."

"And where are you going to take her? Ideally, you need to keep yourself surrounded by people you trust. Staying somewhere secluded will make it too easy for her to find you."

Aubrey muttered something behind him, and it wasn't complimentary. Not that Jackson cared. His only priority was to keep her safe.

"Make sure the higher-ups know the situation, and get some teams out searching for the elusive Ms. Feyer."

Neil sighed. "You say that like I don't know how to do my job. Where are you thinking of going?"

"I'll take her back home with me." Jackson hung up without saying goodbye and turned to face Aubrey, who watched him with wide eyes. "You caught the gist of that?"

"You want me to go home with you? You've got to be kidding me."

"It won't be for long, just enough to stop the jaguar from deciding you'll be a good replacement for what her boss wants." There were other places he could take her. The headquarters would have been a good one or one of the safe houses.

But there was a part of him that liked the idea of taking her home. He hadn't been in a rush to leave her side, not with the connection forging between them. Now, he didn't have to. "I have an event I need to attend; you can be my date."

"Jackson, I don't want to disrupt your life."

"You won't be. You are in danger, and it's our fault." He tapped the bottom of her chin, guiding her face up. Her eyes had started to look more human. Her gaze flickered away from him before they met his again. "Just think of it as a vacation. When was the last time you took one?"

"I haven't. There hasn't been time."

Her reply didn't surprise him, and it was something they both shared. Since joining FUC, he had constantly been busy. There hadn't been much chance to relax.

"Now there's plenty of time. I'll let Alyce know someone has been in your office. She's going to be pissed to find out someone trespassed on Academy grounds."

Aubrey was about to protest, but he placed a finger on her lips, stopping her.

"It's for the safety of the cadets and the other residents of the Academy. No one knows about this place, and if anyone finds out how important it is, that could change everything." The Academy would have to be abandoned and restarted somewhere new.

She stepped away from him. "Fine, but I need to go home and pack some clothes."

He got the distinct impression she didn't like being told what to do. Two sides warred inside of her, the demure mouse and something more primal. Intrigued didn't even begin to cover how he felt about her.

He liked her, and if his lion was right, she was their mate.

It wasn't going to be easy on them. For one, Aubrey hadn't reached the same conclusion as him, or if she had, she wasn't telling. Then, there was his mother. Cassandra Holt wasn't going to like the pairing, since it wouldn't result in purebred cubs.

"I'm going to pack some things up here, from my office, that I want to take home. I also need to leave a message for the other librarians."

Jackson gave her a lazy smile, even if he felt anything but. Every nerve was on a razor's edge, but his poker face had always been unreadable.

"And I'll go see security. You've got ten minutes to grab what you want."

"And what if it takes longer?"

"Then I'm going to come back and carry you off the campus over my shoulder."

She gasped against his lips as he stole another kiss. Suddenly she stepped away from him, her cheeks flushed and her breath heavy.

"Unless you want to see if I'll follow through, you'll be quick," he warned, turning away and leaving his mate flustered. The word *mate* didn't terrify him in the slightest.

Marking her, claiming her, was the surest thing in his world.

CHAPTER TEN

IF she had known FUC would uproot her life, would she still have helped them? Probably. It had nothing to do with the mind-blowing sex with Jackson... Okay, maybe it had a little to do with that. But it also had to do with the fact that she had finally been able to fulfill a dream of hers. For a short amount of time, she had been a part of FUC.

Now she was pulling up next to Jackson Holt's suburban home while he filled the awkward silence with idle chitchat that she mostly ignored.

Her brain was focused on other things.

Mate.

There it was again, the barest of whispers and a word that terrified her. It couldn't be true. Who had ever heard of such a pairing? Predator and prey, it shouldn't have even been an option. There was no way he could feel the same way. It had to be her touch-starved state.

When was the last time someone had held her? Or cared for her? She was drawing connections that weren't even there.

"I'll grab your bag." Jackson opened his door and stepped out.

"I can get my bag," she snapped as she got out and looked around. A mostly deserted street, with people mowing their lawns and drinking on their decks. "I didn't picture you living in a place like this."

"And where did you think I'd live?" He closed the trunk.

"You're a Holt." Aubrey shrugged, like that was the only explanation she needed.

She waited for him to join her again as she looked around. A porch and a slightly overgrown garden—she doubted he had much time to tend to it with all his work with FUC. The garden was a brilliant mishmash of colors, but mostly reds and blues, which worked perfectly together. Whoever he had hired to tend the garden had good taste.

"I'm as much my parents as you are yours." He walked past her and up the steps onto the porch, unlocking the door and gesturing her inside. "I can live anywhere I want, and I've always wanted to get away from the busy city streets. The life of an agent is hectic at the best of times. Some days you just want peace. Do you understand?"

The thing was she did. There might have been a part of her that craved adventure, a life denied to her, but she knew the peace in stillness. "How long am I supposed to stay with you?"

"A few days. Shouldn't be much longer than that." He closed the door behind him and walked down the hallway.

And where was she supposed to sleep? She followed him into another room. A bedroom. The king-sized bed had a brown headboard, which matched the color of the drawers on either side of it. There was a large dark blue circular rug underneath it. Jackson put her bag on the bed. She didn't move from the door. The whole situation was going to take some time to adjust to. He turned around, ran his fingers through his hair, and smiled.

"This is your room," she surmised.

"I figured we could share," he said, his smile fading. For a second, he looked confused. "I promise I won't steal all of the covers."

She still hadn't moved from her spot. "What's going on between us?" Aubrey finally asked, looking down at the wooden floorboards. This wasn't a conversation she wanted to have, but it was one they needed to have.

"You know what's going on." He moved in front of her, and she let him raise her chin until their gazes locked. His eyes flickered to her mouth. "You feel it too, don't you? I want you."

Pleasure shot down to her core, and she clamped her thighs together. The rumble of his voice caressed her skin like a physical touch. There had to be more than just that, but she wasn't brave enough to say the words.

He leaned forward, and she held her breath as he kissed her. He touched her waist and tugged her toward him. Aubrey stumbled, but he held her steady. With his lips on the curve of her neck, she sighed. Why couldn't it always be this way?

It could be.

She mentally squashed the words. No, it wasn't love, just pure carnal desire. She needed to accept that before she ended up getting hurt.

"Aren't we supposed to be doing something today?" she asked, trying to refocus them both.

Jackson swore underneath his breath. "You're right. Knowing my mother, she knows I'm back in town. I better call her, make sure she doesn't make an impromptu visit." His cold fingertips against her exposed skin made her shiver. "Though if you keep moving like that, we're not going to be leaving my bed."

As he waited for his mother to answer her phone, he double-checked his fridge. FUC had put a target on Aubrey's back, even if it was unintentional. It was his fault for going to visit her, though. Layla could have been following him and then figured out who Aubrey was. There was no way to know for sure. He only hoped taking Aubrey away from the Academy would keep her safe.

"You're back in town?" his mother answered.

"Yes," he said through gritted teeth. Why couldn't she be a *normal* mother? He knew it hadn't been easy on her since his father's death. But had she always been so cold? "I thought I'd let you know before you sent members of the pride to come and find me."

Jackson might have made the decision not to take over the company, but that didn't mean he wasn't still an alpha. Anyone who tried to come after him would regret it. The only reason he didn't lose his shit with his mother was respect, something she hadn't earned.

"You're being dramatic." His mother sighed—reminding them both that *she* was the dramatic one of the family. "Anyway, I'm happy you're back from your mysterious little trip. I can start putting some plans into action."

A growl built in the back of his throat. His worry about Aubrey was making his hold on his temper tenuous. "The party isn't for a couple of days." By the sounds of it, she hadn't stopped with her ridiculous plans for him to give her an heir.

"I've been meeting with some lovely ladies. All from well-connected families. I'm sure you'll be pleased."

Jackson rubbed his forehead. "I don't need your help with finding someone." He cleared his throat. "I'm bringing a date."

For a long second, his mother didn't reply. "Not that I don't trust you, dear, but it's probably for the best if I do the matchmaking. I also need you to come into the office and sign some paperwork."

"I'll make some time for that, but"—he gripped his phone so hard the plastic cracked—"I'll be bringing Aubrey with me, or I don't come at all. What will it be, Mother?"

Did she plan on fighting him about this? He honestly didn't know. No, the event was too important, and people would talk if Jackson didn't make an appearance.

"What family is she from? I'm assuming she's a lioness." There was a long, drawn-out pause as she waited for an answer. "Jackson?"

"Goodbye, Mother, we'll see you soon." He didn't wait for her reply before he hung up. He had taken Aubrey out of a potentially dangerous situation and placed her into another one. Jackson didn't think his mother would hurt her, but he knew she wouldn't approve. She certainly wouldn't think a mouse was a good mate for a lion.

Neither of them had much choice in the matter, though. Nobody had any control over who they were mated with. The pull was too strong, too overwhelming to be ignored. It was a connection that could only be severed by death.

He glanced over his shoulder, back toward his bedroom. Aubrey hadn't emerged yet, and there weren't any sounds of movement. When he popped his head around the door to see if she was all right, he found her on the bed.

Her eyes were closed, strands of wild brunette hair splayed out on his pillow while she curled up on her side

—fast asleep. The sight eased a tightness in his chest. It was like he had discovered something he hadn't even known was missing.

They would need to talk about their future soon. There was a chance she didn't even feel the connection, or if she did, she didn't believe it.

A lion and a mouse. The fates had a twisted sense of humor.

CHAPTER ELEVEN

It didn't take Aubrey long to remember where she was. Jackson's scent covered every inch of the bed, making her ache with need. She rolled onto her back, not in any rush to leave the bedroom.

What was she supposed to do now? Usually, at this time, she would be at the Academy, sorting through late returns and replacing them on the shelves.

She hadn't even called her parents to tell them what was happening. When was the last time she'd seen them... a few years back? They hadn't approved of her decision to work for the Academy. *Why can't you work for a normal library?* That had been the common question and one she couldn't understand.

She wasn't normal. None of her family were. They could shift into rodents, bigger than the average ones—though not Miranda-sized, more like large dog sized—whenever they wanted to for the love of God. Why were they eager to forget that? Because they weren't as important in the shifter hierarchy? A wave of familiar anger surged through her, and she closed her eyes, taking deep breaths. She touched the empty side of the bed. Cold. Wherever Jackson had slept, it hadn't been with her.

Eventually, she found him in the kitchen, shirtless, in a pair of low-slung joggers that highlighted the muscles in his back. For a split second, she thought about dashing into the bathroom and brushing her hair, certain she looked like she'd been dragged through a hedge backward.

Just as she was about to do that, he turned, and the smile he flashed her extinguished any fears she had at the moment. In the light of day, he looked better than anyone had any right to look. Broad shoulders and a narrow waist, with muscles she hadn't even known had existed before knowing him.

He looked good enough to eat.

"Morning." Light danced behind his amber eyes as if he found great amusement in the effect he had on her. "My eyes are up here, sweetheart."

Her face went hot. "You're enjoying this, aren't you?"

He brought his steaming cup to his lips and took a sip. "It isn't the worse feeling in the world, knowing you find me desirable."

Aubrey snorted. "I think any woman with a pulse and probably a few men feel the same way. Did you make me a drink?"

Jackson stepped aside and revealed a red mug. She mumbled a thank you as she went to retrieve the coffee. He didn't move from his spot as he watched her with hooded eyes. Any heat that had left her flooded back.

The lion shifter leaned to the side slightly. "You know you're the only one who matters." He kept his voice low, like a growl, and she shivered.

She took her cup back to the safety of the table. He still hadn't moved from his place at the counter, but there was something about him, an energy that filled the entire room. "What are we doing today?" she asked, swiftly changing the subject.

"The party we need to attend is formal. I thought I'd buy you some clothes."

"You want to take me shopping?" She sat down and blinked a few times. When did she end up in the twilight zone? A lifetime of being given only the barest of attention and now she had a mountain of a man completely focused on her. It was going to take some getting used to. "I brought a dress, since you'd mentioned something about a party."

In all honesty, she hadn't been paying attention. Her office had been ransacked. The thought of having someone in her private sanctum made her skin crawl. The overwhelming urge to shift had nearly overtaken her. That was why he had found her on the floor, doing the exercises her therapist had taught her.

"Besides, aren't there more important things you should be doing?"

"I need to pop into the office." He shrugged, and the joggers dropped a little lower, revealing a bit more of the deeply carved V below his abs.

"I didn't know you ran the company."

"I don't. My mother's the one in charge. I'm just the figurehead, but that doesn't save me from signing paper-work. It's one of the downsides of my mother wanting me to take over when she retires." He put his cup down, and for a brief second, Aubrey thought he was about to add something to that, but he smiled tightly at her and changed the subject. "I was hoping you wouldn't have to meet my mother so soon, but I can't leave you here, alone."

"Is she that bad?"

He walked toward her and brushed a kiss against her forehead. The sweet gesture made her heart skip a beat. He pulled her into a loose hug, and she rested her head against his chest, breathing in his scent. "She's old-fashioned."

"What does it matter? We don't even know what we are yet." *Mate* "I mean, when Layla is captured, I'll go back home, won't I?"

His grip tightened. "That's up to you."

JACKSON HELD THE DOOR OPEN FOR AUBREY AND PLACED his hand near her lower back, guiding her into the lion's den. The company was known for its holdings all over the world. Even if he had no interest in anything they did, his mother made sure he knew enough to get by.

As he walked through the lobby, it felt like a noose was getting tighter around his neck. This wasn't his world. At least his father had understood that. A part of him had been tempted to wear some battered jeans and one of his graphic T-shirts, but he'd slipped into one of his rarely worn suits instead.

Aubrey had dressed in a simple outfit that wouldn't have looked out of place in the library she worked in. Simple trousers and a smart pale-pink blouse, which looked great against her skin.

"Mister Holt." The receptionist stood and smiled brightly at him. "It's a pleasure to see you, sir. Would you like me to inform Mrs. Holt you're here?" The man's gaze flickered to Aubrey. "That you're both here?"

"No, it's fine, Wayne. I'll surprise her."

They took the private elevator up to her office. Aubrey leaned against the wall, arms crossed and gazing at the floor, not looking comfortable in the slightest.

"Are you okay?" he asked.

She gave him a small smile. "If you told me last week I would be out of my safe space and in the city, I wouldn't have believed you."

A pang of regret hit him. "I'm sorry I put you in this situation in the first place."

She bit her bottom lip. "I always wanted to have a little excitement in my life. I wanted to be an agent and see the world when I grew up."

"And what stopped you?"

"Everyone who saw me as prey and not much else."

All he wanted to do was hold her. To whisper in her ear that everything would be okay. Jackson would die for her without a second thought. They belonged together. The elevator came to an abrupt stop, and the doors opened. He offered his hand, and something eased in his chest as she slipped her hand into his. "I don't see you like that."

"And how do you see me?" she asked, her expression coy.

"Beautiful and smart, of course. Now, let's get this out of the way, and I'll take you somewhere less oppressive."

"The prodigal son has returned." Esther, his mother's receptionist, looked amused when she spied him. The lynx shifter had been a regular sight when his father brought him into the office. She kept her dark hair short, and half the strands were pure white. Like Wayne, her focus moved to Aubrey and specifically to their joined hands.

"Hey, Esther, Mother said I had paperwork to sign, and since I'm in town for a bit..."

"You thought you'd grace us with your presence." She rose from her seat and studied his mate. "And who are you?"

"Aubrey. I work at the Academy." Esther looked her over, and his mate visibly straightened. "Do you make a habit of staring? It's not very polite." There was a heat to her words, irritation.

"You're very young to be a teacher."

"I'm a librarian."

"Your mother is going to love her," Esther informed him, smirking without taking her eyes away from Aubrey. "At least she's a shifter."

Then Esther breathed in deeply and wrinkled her nose before she turned her attention to Jackson. "You can't be serious."

He leaned forward and let his lion show in his eyes. "I can't be serious about what, Esther?"

The older woman's face went white.

"Remember who you're talking to before you say whatever's racing through your head." For a split second, he thought she might say something, but she pursed her lips together. "Good."

He gave Aubrey's hand a gentle squeeze.

The Holts were old school. Which was one of the reasons his mother was dead-set on the idea of pairing him with a lioness. She wanted the bloodline to remain pure. Nobody's opinion mattered more than his, and his mind was made up.

Some shifters never found their true mate, and he considered himself lucky to have found her.

CHAPTER TWELVE

THE URGE TO SAY SOMETHING TO THE WOMAN BEHIND THE desk had nearly overwhelmed her. All it had taken was one touch from Jackson for the feeling to pass.

They walked into the office together, a united front for all to see. Another woman was sitting behind a desk, but there was no mistaking who this person was. She held a phone to her ear and faced the window behind the large desk.

Aubrey took the time to look around at the plush dark grey carpet and the beige walls. Against one wall was an extensive bookcase, with sections that held silver-framed photos. Three people, all with amber eyes. The cheeky grin on the young boy told her all she needed to know. Jackson, with his parents. Aubrey didn't know what had happened to his father, but whatever happened, Jackson had been young. The photographs worked as a shrine to a man lost and to happier times.

She looked at Jackson, who smiled at her.

"Yes, the party is this Saturday. I'm just confirming you'll be sending your lovely daughters to see us. I know my son will be thrilled to meet them. There will be a few ladies at the party, all eager for his attention. I suggest they wear their best dresses."

Aubrey froze as his mother's words sank in. She frowned at Jackson, and there was no mistaking the barely contained rage in his eyes. He held himself completely rigid. They hadn't had a conversation about what was happening between them. Was this why? Was she just a distraction before he settled down and got married?

She tried to pull her hand free, but his grip tightened. "I can explain."

Cassandra Holt turned in her seat, placed the phone down, and crossed her arms. She was everything Aubrey's parents had warned her about predators. The look in her eyes was cold and unfriendly as she studied Aubrey, her lips twisted in a sneer.

The woman found her lacking and barely worth any of her valuable time. It wasn't the first time she had been viewed in such a way, and it wouldn't be the last. It took every ounce of her will not to look away.

"I told you I don't need a date for the party." A growl rumbled in Jackson's chest. "What the hell do you think you're playing at?"

"I'm keeping your options open." His mother waved her hand dismissively. "I'm sure Ms. Taylor will make a fine date, but she's not worthy of birthing my grandchildren."

Aubrey sighed. What had Jackson told her? "Your son is protecting me, that's all."

He stilled next to her as his mother looked at her with steely intensity. "Your scents are mingled together. He isn't just protecting you."

His grip loosened, and he stepped toward the seated woman. Power came from him in waves as his animal came to the surface. In the presence of any other predator, Aubrey might have been scared, worried about an attack, but she knew his anger wasn't directed at her.

"I've chosen Aubrey. She's mine, and I'm hers. Don't think you can come between us, Mother. You won't like where it ends up."

If Cassandra was scared, the lioness didn't show it. "I will not have half-breed children brought into this family," she said coldly. "You will pick a wife from the list of women I've chosen."

"Or what? You'll disown me? You already know I don't want to take over the company. There are other options. You just don't want to acknowledge them."

"You will not bring up Celeste or Ethan again." The woman cocked an eyebrow and went back to looking at Aubrey. "Every problem has a solution, Jackson. Maybe you shouldn't be the one to push me."

They traveled back to his home in silence. There were a million problems that raced through her mind, one drifting into another. Nothing stayed still long enough for her to focus on solving it.

Jackson had claimed her, which meant something important. It wasn't just a fling. That nagging thought that had been popping up in the back of her mind since they had been together was true.

She sat in one of the chairs in his living room and kicked off her heels.

Mated with a lion? It had to be a twisted joke.

They weren't compatible in the slightest, but he seemed so sure. What was it like to have such blind faith, especially in something Aubrey found hard to believe?

She closed her eyes and rubbed the bridge of her nose.

"Here, take this."

She looked up to see Jackson holding a glass half-filled with a rich amber liquid. She dutifully took it but stopped short of taking a drink.

"Your mother's a..."

He sat in one of the chairs. "A real piece of work."

"Has she always been like that?"

The usually playful lion shifter looked weary. "When my father died, it changed a lot of things."

Aubrey curled her legs up and rested her chin against the palm of her hand. "And they were true mates?" Her parents had been mates, and she couldn't think of anyone more perfect for the other. It was a shame that acceptance hadn't been allowed to her.

Jackson nodded. "You hear horror stories about what happens when someone's mate dies. How the loss breaks the other person. I think my mother closed a part of herself off. Like flipped a switch and stopped the emotions from overwhelming her." He rubbed his bottom lip, deep in thought. "I don't know her anymore. She certainly isn't the mother I remember."

"Did you mean what you said?" Aubrey sipped the amber liquid. She didn't make a habit of drinking alcohol. The idea of not being in control terrified her, but if there was ever a day that called for alcohol, it was today.

The corner of his lips kicked up into a smile. "Which part?"

Was he going to make her say it? At least some of the light had returned to his eyes. "The claiming part." As soon as the words left her, it was like a weight had been lifted from her chest. "You know what that means, right?"

He nodded. "You're my mate."

And suddenly, there was no way to take the words back. They could have skirted around the issue, pretended it didn't exist, and simply recognized it as something foolish. Now they couldn't do that. "How can you be so sure?"

He moved from his chair and knelt in front of her. She held herself still as he reached out, brushing his palm against her cheek. "Because I can feel it. For once, I'm in total agreement with my lion. He knows how important you are to me. He feels the same way about your animal." Aubrey's closed her eyes and leaned into his touch.

"You know how insane this sounds. A lion and a mouse?"

"There are plenty of unique pairings in the world. Why should we be any different?" Suddenly his hands were on her waist, and she was pulled from the chair and into his lap. A shiver went down the curve of her spine as he nuzzled her neck.

"You smell so good," he said as she put her arms around his neck, and he kissed the soft skin there. "You feel the same way, don't you?"

Every part of her wanted to shout from the rooftops that she felt the same way. A lifetime of feeling she was alone and that she'd always be that way had hardened her. Now she had a man who wanted her, who held her as if she was made from fragile glass.

"I can't say it." She rested her forehead against his. "I'm sorry."

"Are you scared?"

The words hit her like a punch to the gut. They barely knew each other, but he could see through every one of her defenses. His tone wasn't mocking—like he found her discomfort amusing—but caring.

Her eyes burned hot with tears. Aubrey nodded, and Jackson cupped both sides of her face, watching her as trails of tears dripped down her cheeks. He brushed them away.

"You don't have to fear this. Nothing in this world means more to me than you."

———

THEY ENDED UP LYING NEXT TO EACH OTHER ON THE plush carpet. She was still asleep when he woke and reluctantly pulled away from her. When he lifted her, her eyelids flickered slightly, but she must have sensed she was safe because she didn't fully wake.

Jackson carried her to the bedroom, laid her down, and pulled covers over her.

"Stay with me," she murmured.

He had wanted to call Neil for an update, but instead, he joined Aubrey under the covers.

Jackson placed a hand on her hip and watched her. A small smile appeared on her face, even if her eyes were still closed. He didn't know the precise moment they started to kiss. Aubrey scooted closer to him, only stopping when their bodies touched and their lips met in an explosive kiss.

She placed a hand at the back of his neck and held him in place as he growled. God, he loved when she took control. "Are you fond of your shirt?" he asked.

She shook her head. Without another word, he grabbed the fabric and tore it apart. At the rate they were going, he would need to replace her entire wardrobe.

He cupped her bra-covered breasts, teasing her nipples with a flicker of his thumbs. She frantically unbuttoned her trousers, kicking them off. Jackson didn't even know if they hit the floor or they were lost somewhere in the bed. It didn't matter. His need to touch her overrode common sense or practicality.

Was this what it was like when someone found their true mate? An undeniable need to touch them. To claim them. He buried his head into the crook of her neck, kissing her there as she moaned his name. She reached between their bodies, unzipped his jeans, and grasped him.

"Fuck," he growled as he clasped her chin. He stopped short of kissing her as she worked her hand up and down his length. A mischievous look had entered her eyes. "You're enjoying this."

"Can't say it's a hardship to know you find me desirable," she replied with a smirk. His own words had come back to haunt him. Aubrey shifted out of his grasp as he leaned back in the bed. She continued to work his hard length, and he barely had any warning as her hand was replaced with her mouth.

Jackson squeezed his eyes shut as his hips buckled. She was amazing. Not just in the way her mouth teased him but in everything she did.

He flipped the bedsheets off and spread his legs to make

it easier for her. She moved into the spot he created for her and looked up at him. The tip of his cock bounced against her lips. He was completely at her mercy, in a way he had never submitted to anyone else. She used both hands to work his length, sucking on his overly sensitive head.

"Fuck, just like that. If you keep going, I'm going to explode inside your mouth. Is that what you want?"

Aubrey didn't answer him, but she didn't stop either. He tried to be careful, but his control was slipping. He thrust upwards as she worked him faster. Jackson reached down and moved her hair away from her face, holding it. Everything was too much, the sounds, the look in her eyes as she sucked, licked, and teased him.

His orgasm surged through him with the speed of a freight train. She swallowed everything he had to give to her, and when he was done, she crawled up the line of his body and lay down, her head against his chest.

They didn't have to say anything. Jackson kept her close, only holding on to wakefulness until her breathing evened out and she fell asleep.

CHAPTER THIRTEEN

Aubrey curled up on her side.

Mate. There it was again. An inner voice she couldn't ignore anymore.

After the rough and explosive moment they shared, they had woken in the middle of the night, and the sex had given way to lovemaking that held a sweetness she had never experienced before. She felt loved and worshipped as he explored every inch of her body. There wasn't a part of her he hadn't kissed or caressed.

She'd never known what it was like to be fully accepted for who she was. In point of fact, she rarely shifted, having denied that part of herself after all the teasing about being prey. Then her parents wanted to pretend they were all normal, even if they weren't. Those times had affected her when she'd been a kid.

Then the years with the therapist to help control her temper.

After a while, it became clear that she wasn't going to fall back asleep. She turned slightly and brushed a soft kiss against Jackson's shoulder before she got out of bed. She slipped on her dressing gown and walked to the kitchen to make a cup of coffee.

If she hadn't been recruited to help with the Budapest assignment, her path never would have crossed with his again. Then she would have resigned herself to a life of being alone. Her dating life was non-existent. It had never bothered her before. It was a life she had already resigned herself to.

It wasn't over, though. Would Layla find out where she was and take her away from Jackson? She found it hard to believe the information in her head was worth the trouble.

Suddenly, Jackson's phone burst to life on the kitchen table. She peeked at it, curious. Neil's name flashed on the screen. Without a second thought, she answered it.

"Hello?"

For a brief second, there was a stunned silence. "Aubrey, is that you?"

"Jackson's asleep. Do you need me to wake him?"

"I'm already awake." Jackson's gruff voice from the doorway startled her. "Put it on speaker," he told her as he went to make his drink. Yesterday morning he had worn joggers, but today he was in the boxers he'd slept in. The sight was spectacular in all the best ways.

Aubrey did as he asked. "What's up, Neil?"

"I wanted to give you an update. We haven't been able to track Ms. Feyer in Budapest. The higher-ups believe she's back in the US. We're going to be sending agents to keep an eye on you, just in case Layla decides to make a grab for Aubrey."

"What do you want us to do?"

"We have a plan, but I can guarantee you're not going to like it."

Aubrey cradled her cup. The wonderful afterglow of sex had faded, and a chill had set into her bones. "You're a real mood killer."

The wolf shifter chuckled over the phone. "I'm a joy to be around. Life and soul of any party I'm lucky enough to be invited to. And speaking of parties. We're going to need you to attend your mother's party, Jackson. We're hoping that'll draw Layla out."

The silence dragged for a moment as Neil's words sank in. "You mean you want to use her as bait? No," Jackson snapped. "That's a terrible idea. Come up with something else."

"We'll do it," Aubrey said at the same time, and Jackson looked at her in surprise. "I'm not going to spend the rest of my life looking over my shoulder, and she's dangerous, Jackson. She knows where the Academy is, even if she might not realize what it is yet. She has to be dealt with."

Aubrey sounded a lot braver than how she felt. Neil made noises of agreement, but she knew she wasn't fooling Jackson. He'd easily hear the tremor in her voice and how her heart pounded.

"I trust you to keep me safe," she said softly. "But I shouldn't be expected to live my life this way. Nobody should."

"I'll bring some equipment over later." There was a click, and Neil was gone.

As Jackson stalked away from his freshly made cup of coffee, Aubrey didn't move. She wasn't scared of him, but it was obvious he expected to be obeyed when he said "no" to the plan. Alphas always did.

She took a drink. Was she ready to do this, to put herself at risk? It wasn't even a question. She would do whatever it took to get her life back to normal. While she liked the time she spent with Jackson, and deep down, she knew they were destined to be together, his home wasn't hers. Hers was at the Academy, and she wasn't ready to give that up for anyone.

Even her mate.

How could she put herself at risk like that, like her life didn't matter?

Jackson growled in frustration. This was all his fault. If he hadn't gone to visit her, then she never would have appeared on Layla's radar. Now his mate was in the crosshairs.

We can keep her safe, his lion told him. *How can you doubt that?*

He rubbed his forehead. Arguing with himself wouldn't help.

"Jackson?" He didn't turn around at the sound of her voice but kept looking out of the window.

Aubrey came up behind him, putting her arms around his waist and resting her head against his back. She wasn't a fighter, and that terrified him. If the shit hit the fan, she wouldn't be able to protect herself. Her hands looked impossibly small against his chest, and he covered them with one of his.

"Are you okay?" he asked.

"Not really," she informed him with a sigh. "But we don't have a choice."

"We always have a choice."

"No, we don't. For all we know, Layla won't even come after me. We might be worrying about nothing."

"Aubrey, if that was true, she wouldn't have ransacked your office. She's done some horrible stuff, and I don't want her to get her grimy paws on you." He could talk to his mother about upping the personal guards at the event. Only someone stupid or desperate would try to kidnap someone from the Holts' seat of power. "I don't like this."

"I know you don't, big guy. How long do we have before we go?"

"Thirteen hours. Neil will be here in ten." His lion mentally paced inside of him. "I'm going to need to shift and get rid of some of this tension. When was the last time you did it?" She stilled behind him. "Aubrey?" He turned around to face her, looking down into her dark eyes. Her gaze flickered away from him.

"A couple of months, but it could be longer."

Now he was confused. "That doesn't make any sense. Why haven't you?"

She made to step away from him, but he touched her shoulders, stopping her. "I don't want to talk about it." There was a finality to her words, and he suspected if he pushed her on the subject, it would end in an argument. But there was still one thing he had to make sure she knew.

"You know I accept every part of you, right?" She didn't answer him, but she also didn't meet his eyes. "Come on. I'm going to take you somewhere."

***

HE DROVE HER OUT IN HIS TRUCK. BEING SURROUNDED BY humans meant there weren't many places he could shift safely. Someone discovering a four-hundred-pound lion in the local area was the quickest way to end up on the news. The forest wasn't densely packed with trees, but going to the center was enough to take them off the beaten path. Also, thanks to the early hour, they wouldn't be discovered. She hadn't said anything in the truck. Her hands were in the pockets of her trousers and her gaze on the ground.

"Can you sense anyone?"

Her brow furrowed slightly, and she closed her eyes. "No."

Jackson hung his jacket on a low-hanging branch and pulled his T-shirt off. Then he unbuttoned his jeans, pushed them off, and placed them with his other items of clothing. He stretched, and Aubrey giggled. "You like what you see?"

"You know I do."

"Bring my clothes." He let the change come over him, and after a moment, he took the shape of his lion. He padded over to her. In this form, his senses were even more acute. The way her unique scent mingled with his was glorious. He knocked his head against her hip. *Follow me.*

CHAPTER FOURTEEN

IT WAS LIKE A FAIRY TALE. A PRINCESS WHO WAS BEING LED somewhere by a majestic beast. Except Aubrey knew the lion who walked by her side. Absentmindedly she trailed her fingers across his coarse fur. Touching him quieted the voices in her head. She wanted to forget about the party later and bask in a moment so perfect it didn't even feel real.

"Where are you taking me?"

He nudged her legs, and she nearly stumbled.

"Okay, it was a stupid question. I know we can't talk this way." There was a rumble of what could have been agreement. If anyone had told her a couple of months ago she would be in a forest with a predator, she would have laughed. If they had told her one of the hottest cadets from the Academy was her mate? She would have handed them her therapist's card. Though he wasn't a cadet anymore. He was a full-blown agent, and he had helped to save the shifter world more times than she could count. And he was hers. And even if she was scared to say the words out loud, she was his.

Suddenly the ground sloped, and she would have lost her footing if Jackson hadn't steadied her. The trip would have been easier in her animal form, but the thought terrified her. For all his words of accepting every part of her, she didn't believe it. Not really.

She stroked his mane, paying attention to his ears. He purred loudly, and she laughed. "Are we nearly there?" She had to duck underneath some low branches and stopped in surprise.

It wasn't a large space, but there were several trees that surrounded a pond filled with lily pads. How many people walked through the forest and missed this place? It looked like it hadn't been disturbed by a human hand for years. There was no trace of rubbish on the ground or in the water.

She made her way toward the pond and knelt, skimming the tips of her fingers across it. *Cold.* She shivered.

Jackson joined her, and she watched as he drank his fill. Then he padded away, turned in several circles, and laid down. With one large paw, he tapped the ground. His message was clear. *Join me.*

Aubrey sat on the damp earth, her back pressed against the curve of his body, and she closed her eyes. It was still early, but she enjoyed the warm rays of the sun against her skin. The only time she had found the same level of peace was when she was surrounded by her books.

She scooted down and curled up onto her side. Her giant lion shifter mate made the perfect pillow. "If I didn't have to worry about tomorrow, I could stay here forever."

The words left her as if they had a life of their own. He made a noise of agreement, a rumble, which she felt in her bones.

In the end, Aubrey didn't know how long they stayed in the grove. Time meant little there. Jackson had shifted back into his human form; she caught the look of disappointment in his eyes. Was it because she hadn't been comfortable to shift or because the party loomed on the horizon? It was hard to tell, and she didn't want to be the one to break such a perfect moment.

He quickly dressed, and they headed back to the truck. When they arrived at Jackson's, there was a motorcycle on the curb. A man moved from his seat on the porch as they approached. He had a headful of rich black hair and an easy smile. He wore a dark blue suit with a matching shirt and tie.

"Did you drive here wearing that?"

The man chuckled. "I know where you keep the spare key." Even if she hadn't recognized his voice, she would have known him. Neil Yun hadn't changed over the years.

Jackson gestured at him. "Aubrey, this sorry excuse for a friend is Neil."

Neil clutched his chest. "Words hurt, man."

For all their teasing, it was obvious the two were close. Aubrey didn't have any close friends of her own, and their easy banter made her feel a little envious. The man offered his hand to Aubrey, and she shook it. It was strange to officially meet him for the first time. Like Jackson, she had known of the wolf shifter from the Academy but never actually known him.

"It's nice to meet you." This was the man who had brought her into the mission. Without him, she wouldn't have discovered her mate. She also wouldn't have a target on her back, but she still owed him a lot.

"Likewise, now let's head inside and get you all kitted out before you have to go to the lion's den."

Jackson took one final look in the mirror and readjusted his tie for the hundredth time. If anyone hurt his mate, he'd tear them limb from limb. Rage simmered in the pit of his stomach. He would have liked to believe nobody was stupid enough to try anything at a party where shifters outnumbered humans, but Layla didn't strike him as someone completely sane.

There had been no subtlety in her desire to burn down a whole library to kill him. And he couldn't forget or forgive the shotgun blast to the ass cheek. The fact she was being quiet now, and nobody knew where she was, was its own brand of crazy. He might not have agreed with the plan, but he did know that putting Layla six feet under was the only way to guarantee Aubrey's safety.

He ran his fingers through his hair and gave his reflection a humorless grin. There was a brief knock on the door, and he turned to face Neil. His friend looked almost apologetic. Jackson hadn't told him of his realization about Aubrey, but his mother had been able to detect their scents intermingled together, so he figured his friend had too.

"You know getting involved with her is a bad idea, right?" He could always trust his friend not to pussyfoot around a subject.

"It isn't some meaningless fling," Jackson informed him. "Neil, she's my mate."

He whistled. "You sure?"

"Hard not to be." He leaned against his chest of drawers. Aubrey was sorting out her final changes in the bathroom. "We have to keep her safe. I can't lose her. Not when I've just found her."

Neil crossed his arms. There was a guarded look in his eyes, but he managed a smile. "That shifter isn't going to get anywhere near her. I promise."

Promises were dangerous in their line of business. It was an unspoken rule never to make one.

Suddenly there was a distinctly feminine cough behind Neil, and he stepped aside to reveal the most beautiful sight Jackson had ever seen. The black dress she wore was simple, hitting just above the knee. The curve of her hip and the swell of her chest was perfectly highlighted. Jackson let his eyes drift down the length of her legs to a pair of black high heels.

When he could breathe again, their eyes met. She had clipped up her black hair, but a few strands had already escaped. There were even flashes of gold at her ears. For a second, time seemed to stop. *Gods, she's beautiful.*

A blush rose in her cheeks. "Do I pass inspection? Does Neil's spy necklace match or does it look out of place?"

"Of course it matches, who do you think you're working with here?" Neil said.

All Jackson wanted to do was kick his friend out and worship every inch of Aubrey. He wanted to make her come so many times she couldn't walk straight for a week. "You look stunning."

"You don't look so bad yourself."

"And I look great too, thanks for saying," Neil replied drily.

Jackson pushed off the dresser and patted his friend on the shoulder. "I didn't even know you owned a suit," he said, not taking his eyes away from Aubrey.

"It doesn't get much use," Neil admitted. "Last time was a funeral."

Another reminder the night could go one of two ways. He slipped a hand around Aubrey's waist, loving the way her breath caught at the contact. Even though the heels gave her an extra couple of inches of height, she still only reached the bottom of his chin. They had places they needed to be, but he had no real desire to leave. "We'll meet you there." His friend looked bemused but left without saying another word.

Aubrey studied him with a frown. "I thought we were all leaving together."

He trailed his fingers up the fabric of her dress, not loosening his grip on her. "I like you in this."

A small smile appeared on her face, and some of the tension left her. "I've just spent half an hour doing my makeup. I'm not going to start over from scratch because you want to make out like horny teenagers."

"Who said anything about kissing your mouth?" Jackson slowly dropped to his knees and pushed the hem of her dress up.

CHAPTER FIFTEEN

The ferocity of their lovemaking almost felt like a goodbye. As if he wanted to memorize every part of her just in case the plan went to hell.

Even as they readjusted their clothes, she could still feel his hands on her. The possessive way he had gripped her butt as he speared her with his tongue. She had held on to the dresser for dear life as she was swept up in a wave of endless pleasure.

When they were done, they quickly cleaned up, and then with a satisfied smile on his face, they left Jackson's house and got into the car.

Nerves started to build in the pit of her stomach as soon as the Holt Building came into view. It looked like a shining beacon against the night's sky. Instead of joining the extensive line of cars that were waiting, Jackson took a left and brought them around the back. There was a security guard on duty, a plump man with a round face and thin moustache. He tugged his hat down and picked up a clipboard. Jackson brought the car to a stop and leaned across Aubrey toward her window. The man broke out into a huge grin when he saw him.

"Mister Holt, it's a pleasure to see you. Your usual space has been reserved for you."

"Thanks, Clive." He settled back into the driver's seat as the other man waved them through. Her heightened senses told her the security guard was a shifter, but it didn't give her any more information than that. She couldn't help but look at every shadow as if it were a hiding place for the woman who wanted to kidnap her. Jackson squeezed her leg, the pressure just enough to settle some of her nerves. She wasn't alone. Her mate was by her side and would do whatever he had to keep her safe.

"Don't leave my side." The gentle rumble of his voice sent shivers down her spine.

"You can't be with me all the time. She won't make a move if she thinks I'm too heavily guarded."

"Why are you in such a rush to put yourself in harm's way?" There was a cracking noise as he gripped the steering wheel.

"I'm not. I want this to be over so I can go back home." Even as she said the words, she doubted they were true. Yes, she wanted it to be over, but the library and her quiet, modest home in the middle of nowhere wasn't the only place she wanted to be. "Let's get this over with."

She leaned toward him and brushed a kiss against his cheek. Then she opened the door and stepped out into the fresh night breeze.

Aubrey noticed how Jackson's gaze swept the room. Was he searching for Layla or the other FUC agents? He kept his hand near her lower back as they walked together, the pad of his thumb rubbing against the bare skin on her back, comforting her.

For a moment, it felt like every set of eyes was on them. It was a little intimating. There also seemed to be an air of confusion. Women were whispering among themselves. How many of them were there because Cassandra invited them?

"Where do we need to go first?" Aubrey asked.

"To see my mother," Jackson said with an air of resignation.

She completely understood where he was coming from. She certainly wasn't in any rush to see the lioness. The woman had made her feelings clear; Aubrey wouldn't be a welcomed addition to the family if Jackson officially claimed her as his mate.

"Come on. She'll be somewhere in the middle."

They passed by Neil, who met Aubrey's gaze before shifting his attention back to the woman he'd been chatting with—a stunning redhead with shocking green eyes. Another agent or part of Neil's cover? She didn't know, but it made her happy to know they weren't alone. She had to trust Layla wouldn't even get close before she was discovered.

Cassandra's voice reached them even before they found her. The dress she wore was a brilliant shade of blue that clung to a figure that could have belonged to someone much younger than her. Her blonde hair was short, but the tips were curled, softening the sharp angles of her face.

Next to her stood a man Aubrey had never met, his posture rigid and his hands clasped behind his back. Her guard?

The lioness's gaze narrowed as she spied them. Jackson moved his hand from its place at her back and clasped hers. The move was deliberate. He wanted to show a united front to his mother. The gesture warmed Aubrey's soul.

The older woman brought her wine flute to her red-painted lips and sipped the golden liquid. Then she clicked her fingers. "Someone get my son a drink. What is the point of servers if there isn't one around when you require one?" Her voice traveled across the dance floor. A few more heads turned in their direction. It also didn't escape Aubrey's notice; she hadn't been mentioned at all.

Cassandra stepped toward them, making a move to take her son's arm, to pull him away from her. Anger surged through Aubrey, and instead of shaking it off, she stepped forward. "Your eyesight must be failing you. I mean that's the only logical reason why you would ignore me." She kept her voice low and steady. Losing her temper in front of the powerful shifter wasn't a clever idea.

Jackson chuckled next to her. Did he feel proud of her for standing up to his mother? It wasn't the same as her claiming him, but at that moment, it was all she could do. Aubrey knew there were several ways the night could play out, but she wasn't going to be made to feel unworthy of the man who loved her. The corner of Cassandra's lips twitched.

"I only acknowledge things that are worthy of my attention. You, my dear, are not. You are nothing but a temporary thing in my son's life. A placeholder until he accepts the woman I've chosen for him."

Aubrey clutched her hand into a fist, her nails biting into her palm. Jackson stilled next to her. It would have been easy for him to say something, to defend her, but the shifter world didn't work like that. If someone viewed her as weak, then she would become a target for someone who thought they deserved the powerful lion shifter more.

"Listen here. I love your son. There's nothing you can do to change that, and if you continue to fight this pairing, all you'll do is push Jackson away. Is that what you want?" The urge to punch the woman in the face nearly overwhelmed her. She couldn't win in a fight against her. Maybe if they stayed in human form, but as soon as Cassandra shifted into her lioness, it would be over.

"She's right," Jackson said as he took two wine flutes off the server's tray. "You know how rare true pairings are, and I won't give this up."

His mother, to her credit, didn't show any reaction to the news. Not surprise, not disgust. Had she already seen this coming since their visit to the office?

"Then you won't have the company."

He laughed. "That's not a punishment. We'll talk later, Mother. I'm going to dance with my mate."

JACKSON HAD ALWAYS SHOWN A LEVEL OF RESPECT TO HIS mother. He knew how hard the last few years had been for her. After his father's death, she became colder, shutting herself off. Part of him recognized it as a survival mechanism. When someone in a true pairing died, it wasn't unusual for the mate to die as well. However, it wasn't an excuse for her attitude now.

He sipped some of the wine before placing the glass on the table. Tonight, his mother was the least of his problems. He couldn't split his focus between her and the impending threat of Layla. Would she come in masquerading as a guest, or was she one of the servers? With so many shifters in such a small space, it was next to impossible to pinpoint a specific one. She could have been anywhere.

A quartet played classical music in the farthest corner, and couples were dancing. He plucked Aubrey's untouched drink out of her hand and put it down with his on the table. Then he guided her onto the dance floor. He pulled her into his arms, her body flush against him as they swayed together. Her hair tickled the his chin, but he was more focused on the feel of her body.

It was maddening in the best way.

"Is she here?" she whispered.

"I haven't seen her," he admitted reluctantly. "I've seen plenty of familiar FUC faces, though. Don't worry."

"It's hard not to."

"Maybe we should talk about something else." It wasn't the best of times for the conversation they'd both been putting off, but if it helped to take her mind off things, it was time.

She turned her head, pulling away from him a little to look up into his eyes. A faint blush to her cheeks and her pitch-black eyes told him all he needed to know. "What do we need to talk about?"

"Our future."

She bit her bottom lip. "I like the sound of that. Our future."

"So why are you scared of it?"

He placed his hand on the curve of her hip. Her arms draped over his shoulders. For that moment, they could have been the only two people in the world. A place where there was no impending threat, no mother who didn't like when control was taken from her.

"It's not like I'm scared. I need you to understand that. I've spent my whole life being told I wasn't good enough. That the things I wanted weren't suitable and I should forget about my shifter side. Because I'm a mouse. Are you sure you want to be tied with me forever?"

"You're the only one I want to be with."

"And if our paths hadn't crossed? Would you still make that choice?"

He paused. In all honesty, he never thought he would find his mate to begin with. "I can't answer that question. No one can. We belong together; we're two sides of the same coin. One can't exist without the other. I know my life is difficult and dangerous, but I want to make this work."

"And my life at the Academy?"

He smiled. "You know that I'm not overly attached to my home, right? I'm more than willing to move to be closer to you." Suddenly Jackson stumbled as someone knocked into him. Neil gave him a wolfish grin.

"A woman matching Layla's description just made a run from the lobby. We're in pursuit. Guess she was dumb enough to try."

A wave of relief hit him, and he brushed a kiss against Aubrey's forehead. "See, I told you everything's going to be okay."

CHAPTER SIXTEEN

As soon as she reached the ladies' restroom, she sank into one of the chairs and sighed. Aubrey didn't know how much tension she'd been carrying until she was able to let go of it. Jackson had been talking to Neil when she excused herself. For a brief second, she thought he would join her but had stopped himself.

They found Layla. He didn't need to worry anymore.

Aubrey couldn't get her head around the fact the mysterious woman who had ransacked her office was now on the run. There was no telling how many agents were now on her trail.

Now Aubrey could return home and to her job. And Jackson would come with her. The door to the restroom opened, and she looked up at the intruder. Cassandra stood there, her arms crossed and the look on her face predatory. She was a beautiful woman, even if there was no warmth in her eyes.

"I was hoping I would catch you not by my son's side."

"Is this the moment you threaten me again?" she asked, suddenly tired. Aubrey squeezed her eyes shut and rubbed her forehead with the tips of her fingers. The excitement of the last few days vanished in the wake of the woman's cold stare. "Why don't you like me? It is because I'm a mouse?"

"You'll pollute the bloodline," Cassandra informed her with a distasteful sniff. "Now, what's it going to cost me to get you out of my son's life?"

"Wait a minute, you want to pay me?" She couldn't believe what she was hearing.

"Everyone has a price." Cassandra tapped her fingertip against her wine flute. "I mean I could simply rip your limbs from your body and gnaw on your bones, but I'd rather try this way first. It's far less messy."

Aubrey got to her feet, her rage simmering inside of her. "If you want me out of your son's life, you're going to have to kill me, but you know what I think?"

"What is that?"

"I think you're bluffing. If you murder me to protect your precious bloodline, it will be the quickest way to lose your son." She didn't know if it was bravery or stupidity or a combination of the two, but she stepped toward her.

The older woman sneered. "You aren't as important to him as you think. He might believe you're his mate, but you're not so sure. I mean you can't even say the words yourself."

"He's my mate." The words had barely left her lips when the door swung open again. A part of her thought it might be Jackson, curious to find out what was taking her so long. She didn't expect the black-haired woman with the gun in her hand.

"Look out!" Aubrey cried, but Cassandra didn't have enough time to react.

Layla swung her arm out, connecting the butt of her gun with Cassandra's face. The sound of the crack was enough to make Aubrey wince. She frantically looked around for an exit, but there wasn't any. No, it was just the three of them. Cassandra hit the floor with a thud, and the other woman approached Aubrey.

"Ms. Taylor, I've been looking everywhere for you."

<hr>

Aubrey had gone to the restroom about ten minutes ago. It didn't take women that long to freshen up, did it? Jackson scanned the dancefloor, searching for his mate and, failing that, his mother. When he didn't see either, he knew something was wrong. Neil was talking about going to a bar to celebrate but stopped when Jackson snagged his arm.

"What's wrong?"

"Aubrey should be back by now."

He darted around the dancefloor toward the nearest

restroom. The one Aubrey had been headed to. Without a second thought, he pushed the door open, and it knocked into something on the floor.

Jackson looked down and saw his mother.

"Call it into the team," he shouted to Neil, who was right behind him. "Layla's somewhere on the premises, and I think she has Aubrey. Make sure Heston knows my mother is here."

"I'll head down to the lobby," Neil said.

"And I'll go to the roof," Jackson replied.

"You think she'll try and leave that way?"

He nodded as he started to run. "It's the only place we haven't accounted for. My earpiece is on."

There were thirty floors to the Holt building. The ball room used for the party was on the fifteenth. There was a chance Layla would try to take the elevator, but he had to trust that Aubrey wouldn't make it easy for her kidnapper.

His lion paced restlessly, eager to break through his skin and take control, but Jackson kept it on a tight mental leash. His animal was good in a fight but would give in to its basic instincts without a second thought.

He took the steps two at a time, even as his legs burned from the effort. As he reached the twentieth floor, he spied something on the ground. Without even stopping, he snatched it up: Aubrey's shoe. She had managed to leave a clue for him. It was still warm. He kept running up. Level twenty-two… twenty-six… then suddenly, voices.

"Do you want me to blow this building up? Because I will!"

"You've dragged me up several flights of stairs. It's your fault that I'm not a little faster."

"Jackson, did you hear that?" Neil's voice was in his ear. Jackson kept his mouth shut. There was every chance that Layla would hear him if he tried to talk. "I'll get the team searching for the bombs. We did a sweep earlier in the day, but we'll double back. I'll get back to you as soon as I can."

Jackson took the next couple of steps as quickly as he could, the claustrophobia threatening to creep up. He shoved it down deep. He had no time for fear, not when his mate was in danger.

"This is all that lion's fault." Layla's voice floated down to him again. "I should be on a beach somewhere drinking a cocktail, a reward for a job well done. Not dragging you around."

"Why do you want me so badly?"

There were still sounds of movement on the stairs. Jackson estimated there were another three floors before she reached the top.

"Because of what's in your head," Layla hissed. "Ideally, I would have gotten the book, but the lion threw himself into the river. Then I planned on getting you at your home, but the big brute was with you constantly."

"So, you waited?"

"Couldn't go back empty-handed. Now shut the hell up."

There was more grunting, and Jackson smiled. Sounded like Aubrey was making it as hard as possible for her kidnapper. She was buying him time. Jackson kept low, turned another corner, and ended up with a barrel of a gun pointed directly at his face.

"Hello, handsome."

***

PANIC SHOT THROUGH AUBREY. SHE THOUGHT SHE HEARD someone on the stairwell behind them, which was why she kept talking, hoping to mask their approach. Layla was clever, though, and clasped a hand over Aubrey's mouth.

The bitter taste of sweat against her lips told her all she needed to know. Layla was desperate and nervous. The shifter kept the gun up and waited, and there was nothing Aubrey could do.

Fear kept her rooted to the step as she silently begged whatever god wanted to take pity on her. *Please don't be Jackson. Anyone but him.* Even in the near-dark, she knew her prayers had gone unanswered.

Jackson appeared from around the corner. At some point, he had taken off his tie, and his blond hair looked wilder than usual. How close was he to losing control?

"Let her go," he said, ignoring the gun Layla pointed in his face.

"If I don't bring her in, I'm as good as dead. It's

nothing personal. I just prefer me alive more than either of you."

"We both know you're not leaving here alive," he growled.

There weren't any lights in the stairwell—it appeared she'd shot out the emergency light. One side had a window that looked out onto the cityscape, letting tiny squares of light come in from the building across the road. It was enough to illuminate the familiar shape of her mate. Those amber eyes filled with concern and barely contained rage.

There were only seconds left before Layla pulled the trigger. Aubrey did the only thing she could do. She started to shift. The process wasn't easy, but as her mouth changed, she bit down on Layla's hand with teeth more rodent-like than human.

The woman screamed, pushing Aubrey away from her with a hard shove.

Layla dropped the gun as Jackson leaped for her. There was the sound of clothing being ripped before a piercing scream filled the air. That was all Aubrey heard before everything went dark.

CHAPTER SEVENTEEN

Layla wasn't going anywhere. As soon as his powerful jaws were around her throat, she was dead. Blood still coated his tongue and was smeared across his face, but his lion had no time to bask in the glory of the kill. Not when he worried about his mate.

Jackson shifted back into his human form and found Aubrey's animal—larger than a normal mouse, almost as big as a medium-sized dog, with a long tail and whiskers poking out from her snout—lying still at the bottom of the stairs. A gentle rise and fall of her chest told him all he needed to know. For a long second, he had worried she'd broken her neck when she was pushed.

He collapsed next to her. He knew how hard the transformation must have been for her. Gingerly he reached out and brushed a hand across her side, finding her fur soft and smooth underneath his hand. She had been small in her human form, but her animal side was much more delicate.

"Aubrey?" The mouse's eyes opened, and he carefully picked her up. "I'm going to take you to the medic downstairs and get you looked at. Don't shift back, okay?"

She twitched her nose, and Jackson took that as all the confirmation he needed.

He didn't bother with his clothes. Nakedness had never bothered him before, and it didn't bother him now. All that mattered was making sure Aubrey was okay. As he walked down to the ball room, he was met by several wide-eyed stares.

"Is she okay?" Neil rushed to his side and didn't mention anything about Jackson's lack of clothes.

"Did you find what you were searching for?" He didn't say the word *bombs* out loud, not wanting to scare the partygoers.

"There's nothing here. Maybe she was bluffing?"

That wasn't a risk Jackson wanted to take. He looked down in his arms. He also didn't want to leave Aubrey while he checked.

"I'll take her." His mother walked toward them with an icepack pressed against the back of her head. She handed the icepack to Heston, who was looking annoyed by her side. Jackson knew Heston would be disturbed by the fact that Cassandra had been attacked.

She offered her hands, but Jackson hesitated. "I'm

not going to hurt her; you have my word. Whatever it's worth to you."

"I'll be right back," he whispered to his silent mate before he handed her over. His mother's usually harsh expression softened slightly as she cradled the unconscious dog-sized mouse in her arms.

"Please tell me you killed the woman who attacked me."

"You'll find parts of her in the stairwell," he called as he started to shift back into his animal form. Thirty floors and a million hiding places, but they had to be sure. Neil, in the shape of his wolf, met him by the bottom of the stairwell with three others. Two more wolves—a grey and a dark red, respectively—and a hyena.

It was time to get to work.

OUT OF ALL THE PLACES AUBREY THOUGHT SHE WOULD wake up, on a reclining leather armchair with a soft blue throw draped over her wouldn't have listed in the top ten. She blinked a few times and then realized she knew exactly where she was.

Cassandra's office.

Jackson's mother sat behind her desk, a framed photo in her hand. Aubrey held the blanket to her naked chest. "What am I doing here?"

"Heston found your dress if you want to put it on." The lioness didn't even look away from the photo.

"Where's Jackson?"

"Getting debriefed by the higher-ups at FUC." Her answers were short and to the point.

Aubrey quickly got dressed. Thankfully, her smaller form meant fewer ripped clothes. The hearing device Neil had crafted into the necklace was gone but had served its purpose. "Layla told me there were bombs. That she would detonate them if I didn't go with her."

"I'm aware, but the woman was bluffing. The FUC team searched the building and didn't find anything." Cassandra put the photo down. "Do you remember what you told me in the restroom?"

Aubrey's face went hot as she sat down. "I said a lot of things."

"You truly believe my son is your mate?"

"Yes." She took a deep breath and sighed. "I love Jackson."

The words had been spoken, and there was no way for her to take them back. Not that she wanted to. A foiled kidnapping certainly put things into perspective.

"It's a dangerous thing, love," Cassandra informed her with an unhappy sigh. "I loved his father with all my heart. It destroyed a part of me when he died so sense-lessly. Did Jackson tell you about him?"

She didn't have a clue where the conversation was going. It wasn't that long ago the lioness had been trying to pay her to stay away from Jackson. What had changed? "Not really. I guessed it was a sore subject for him."

"It is," Cassandra admitted. "You're not who I would have chosen for my son."

And there it was, the biting words Aubrey expected from her.

"But that has more to do with me than you."

Suddenly, Aubrey was glad she was sitting down because her legs went weak.

Cassandra continued. "Jackson has never bowed to the expectations of his upbringing. I don't know why I thought now would be any different."

"He's a good man."

The corner of Cassandra's mouth twitched, but it wasn't a scowl. She smiled. "He's the best of men, but don't tell him I said that. I have my reputation to think about after all."

The door opened behind them, and Aubrey rushed to her feet as soon as she saw the familiar amber gaze of the man she loved. With more speed than she thought she possessed, she rushed across the room and into his arms. For a second, his body was tense, but he relaxed against her.

"Are you okay?" He brushed a kiss against her forehead then met her gaze.

She raised onto her tiptoes, not caring they weren't alone, and kissed him. He moaned against her lips, and any doubts lingering in her mind were gone. The perfect way they fitted together, it felt like home.

"I'd rather not see my son make out with his mate like a horny teenager if that's all right with you."

Aubrey's face burned as she stepped away from Jackson. He looked at her with amazement. His eyes practically shone, and then he nodded at his mother. "I'll call you in the morning."

His mother waved her hand dismissively. "I think you have more pressing things to deal with than worrying about me. I'll be fine to wait till Monday. Goodbye, Aubrey. I'm sure we'll see each other again soon."

And with that, the intimidating lioness turned her attention back to the photo she had been looking at.

It had been one hell of a night. From what Layla had said—or rather, what she hadn't said—they had the impression that she didn't know about the Academy. She had been more focused on getting Aubrey as a consolation prize for not getting the book.

There was no telling how much information whoever Layla worked for had, but there was every chance they didn't have much.

Aubrey was safe, for now. It was like a huge weight had been lifted off his shoulders, and hearing his mother acknowledge Aubrey as his mate was the icing on the cake.

There hadn't been any need for words. As soon as the door was closed behind them, they were out of their clothes in the blink of an eye. They hadn't even made it to the bed. He'd taken her against the hallway wall then bent over the kitchen counter. Then they had stopped to refuel at his fridge.

Her dark hair was a wild mess, and neither of them bothered with clothes. His lion had roared with approval as she fed him some grapes. The only thing sweeter was the nectar at the crux of her legs. A place he planned on feasting on soon.

"God, you're beautiful."

She blushed, and he loved the way the pinkish glow spread down to her chest. "You don't have to keep saying that."

"You should never doubt it," he said as he plucked a grape and fed it to her. "I should have told you something earlier. I know you want to return home, but FUC has offered you a job. I mean if you're interested."

"What's the job?"

"Looks like they need a little help in deciphering Miklos Bathory's book. It's taking them too long, and they believe hiring you will cut the time in half. What do you say. Do you want the chance to study some long-forgotten text?" Aubrey squealed happily and threw her arms around him. "You won't even have to move. The higher-ups have decided to let you study the book at the Academy. And I've been assigned to stay with you if you'll have me."

Aubrey pulled away from him, and her eyes shone brightly. "I love you, Jackson."

"I love you too."

The End.

Or is it? There are still lots of mysteries to be solved! Who did Layla work for, and why do they want Bathory's research? Neil Yun is all over it in the next book, *The Wolf's Vixen*, coming in November 2022!

And there are more FUC Academy books from other authors coming your way soon!

To find out more about these books and more, visit worlds.EveLanglais.com or sign up for the EveL Worlds newsletter. If you haven't already downloaded the **free Academy intro** (written by Eve Langlais) make sure you grab it at worlds.evelanglais.com/wordpress/book/fucademy1!

ABOUT THE AUTHOR

Samantha Allard has always wanted to be a writer. She spent her teenage years reading books and scribbling notes on napkins. Now she's older, perhaps not any wiser, and getting her stories published. Young adult, steampunk or fantasy. The genre doesn't matter as long as the story is told.

She can be found in her office most days. Others she trapped at the dreaded day job.

goodreads.com/9792435.Samantha_Allard

facebook.com/samanthaallardwriter

instagram.com/samanthaallard_writer

The Wolf's Vixen

This sly fox is eyeing the henhouse, but a handsome wolf is blocking her score.

Elizabeth "Lizzie" Adams has always lived outside the shifter world, taking on jobs that allowed her to sneak around in her fennec fox form without humans becoming wise to her. But when her sister is threatened, she joins the Furry United Coalition Newbie Academy under false pretenses.

Wolf shifter Neil Yun is adjusting to life as a solo agent. He misses being part of a dynamic duo, but fate has a surprise in store for him when his mate sits down next to him on his international flight back to Canada. Lizzie is sweet and sexy,

but she's hiding something and he's determined to sniff it—
and her—out.

Lizzie knows an upstanding FUC agent like Neil couldn't be
serious about someone like her. Someone who works outside
the law. Especially when he learns how she's used him to gain
access to the Academy.

Can the crafty fox keep the wolf at bay, or will he howl his
way into her heart before it's too late?